WELC(RICHARD S. SHAVER'S CIRCLE OF FRIENDS

Here in book three of "The Shaver Mystery" you're going to be meeting a wide variety of other-worldly characters. First, there's Nydia, Shaver's beautiful, blind soul-mate who introduces him to the ancient life-recordings of many of Lemuria's most famous people, like Bar Mehat, a grizzled tough warrior and descendant of Thor. Later on you'll meet "Lord" Bonur Golz, who's not unlike a common Mafia boss! Keep your eyes on Lura, she was a woman of great beauty who was called upon to entertain the "evil ones." You might remember Mutan Mion from "I Remember Lemuria." He was, a human who became a Titan 1000 years ago and shares his story of Lemuria.

Then of course, there's Shaver, himself, the central character of "Thought Records of Lemuria." And when you read Shaver's letters to the readers, you'll find yourself running head-on into a mental brick wall!

TABLE OF CONTENTS

THE SHAVER MYSTERY

Book Three

By
RICHARD S. SHAVER

ARMCHAIR FICTION
PO Box 4369, Medford, Oregon 97504

*For more information about Armchair Books and products, visit our
website at...*

www.armchairfiction.com

Or email us at...

armchairfiction@yahoo.com

Everybody Loves Ray Man

—Foreward to Book Three—

When we first decided to publish books one and two of *The Shaver Mystery*, we did it because we felt Richard S. Shaver should have his own special venue. I had originally intended to stick Shaver's tales in our double novels here and there, but after reading *The Red Legion* (included in Book One) I realized that the average sci-fi reader—without being properly prepared—would probably read a chapter or two and say, "What in the *hell* am I reading?" Thus, we made the rather sweeping decision to put the majority of Shaver's works into standalone *Shaver Mystery* volumes, which we feel will more properly showcase his unique, over-the-top style of fiction(?) So here it is, Book Three of *The Shaver Mystery*. You're getting two of Dick Shaver's wackiest novels, *Thought Records of Lemuria* and *The Masked World*, plus other goodies, too. Both novels will take you deep into Shaver's "mad" worlds, which will lead you not only into Earth's under-worlds, but deep into unknown regions of outer space as well.

When reading Richard Shaver's "true account" stories, you will notice that they are literally filled with various kinds of "rays." As you read on (undoubtedly with a smile on your face—or perhaps a look of complete puzzlement) you'll find that Shaver believed that all of us surface people are constantly being bombarded with various kinds of rays from ancient machines, still operating from deep inside the Earth. These rays are both good and bad depending on whether or not a *dero* (bad guy) or a *tero* (good guy) is operating the machinery. So here's a helpful list of just some of the delightful rays you'll be reading about soon:

"will" rays	ben rays	black, shorter rays
ancient pleasure rays	beneficial rays	blue absorptive rays
automatic fire rays	black rays	carbon rays

conductive rays
control rays
dero rays
destructive rays
detrimental rays
devil rays
disintegrating rays
dis-rays
dissolving rays
distance-rays
double rays
erasing rays
fecund rays
fire-extinguisher rays
great old rays
Grindel-Mathew rays
invisible rays
ionizing rays

loyal rays
luminosity rays
mad rays
medical rays
mind current rays
nerve rays
nomad rays
nose-rays
offensive rays
old miracle rays
pain rays
penetra rays (or
penetrays)
police rays (*I got a
ticket from one of those
the other day!*)
precipitating rays
private rays

rodite-rays
sane rays
secret rays
seeing rays
space-rays
stim-rays
subtle rays
super-stimulator rays
telaug rays
tele rays
unknown friendly
rays
visi-rays
vis-rays
war-rays
watch rays
weapon rays
wind-rays

One wonders if Shaver's editor, Raymond A. Palmer ever really believed any of this. Palmer loved this kind of stuff and was truly the P. T. Barnum of pulp mags. Just what kind of relationship did the two have? Palmer was known to have poker games with his regular contributors to *Amazing* and *Fantastic Adventures.* Can you imagine Shaver sitting around a poker table with Palmer, Don Wilcox, Dave Reed, Bob Bloch, and others? Imagine Palmer exploding into a rage when he discovered that his pal, Shaver was using his "I've-got-invisible-eyes-floating-behind-you-and-can-see-what-cards-you're-holding-ray."

By the way, there's a terrific interview with Palmer on You Tube. Search the words: Shaver, Mystery, Palmer. It's amazing!

So read on, my friends. Rays, mechs, telaugs, deros, teros, and more are waiting for you in the lost worlds of R. S. Shaver.

−Greg Luce
Editor-in-chief,
Armchair Fiction

Open Letter to the World

January 18, 1945
To My Fellow Men:

I, Richard Shaver, want your attention. I must get to you somewhat of the knowledge I have gained in strange ways; so that the mighty hidden wisdom I have unearthed does not perish with me, but becomes instead a part of the general living mind of man. If you have intelligence you will read between the lines of my writings of what may seem at first glance to be the wildest fiction, and find certain immediately useful information as well as the answers to age-old puzzles such as apparently occult and spiritual phenomena; things men fear to speak of but know are true; terrible agonies; hidden and secret pleasures spoken of only as "forbidden fruit"; ways of life that powerful and often foolish social and religious organizations have hidden since earliest times because of a worm-like fear of things they could not quite understand.

Such students will be able to read between the lines of my stories and in their minds build a true picture of the life-that-was in ancient, unwritten-of days. They will realize that I have indeed fathomed many a great-lost secret of power such as the medieval sorcerers who, for fear of being burned at the stake, wrote of in obscure codes. Even you who read this tale as fiction will assuredly sense within yourselves the stirring of something that will whisper and call to you to seek further.

The things of which I write will be touched upon in literature more and more frequently in the future by students who realize that mankind should be wakened, even if rudely, to the realities underlying surface life; since those realities wield more influence upon Earth people than is generally known, even to the average student of secret things.

Abraham Merritt, in "The Snake Mother," "The Face In The Abyss," "The Moon Pool" and other of his tales, has given those of us who know and seek for more information of the hidden ways of life, some of the secrets of the antique mechanisms and their hidden places of concealment. Yet I think he did not know that these caverns lie in a great network under all of Earth's surface and are actually still inhabited by wretched descendants of the Ancient Ones. His books betray to me certain lacks in his information which I will attempt to make up for the sake of those who seek the truth about these ancient, unspoken-of remnants of the vast super-science so ably described as the property of the Snake Mother.

For instance, in "The Snake Mother," Lantlu and his followers are evil, but retain their beauty and a certain cleverness as well as the method of eternal life. But in the actual life in the caverns today, the evil ones are neither beautiful nor clever nor do they live much longer than normal men. The more intelligent, well-meaning members of these cavern people are sometimes as beautiful and all-wise as Merritt's immortals, but although they have some knowledge of the methods of the Ancients to obtain near-immortal existence, they are not able to use the methods effectively because of their constant struggles with the degenerate, evil members of the race.

Among those remnants of the Ancients there has been degeneration to a degree that would seem incredible did not the creatures still exist, living proofs of the efficacy of the ancient generators of beneficial life force. For in no other way than by constant flows of beneficial force from those indestructible mechanisms could such manifestly unfit creatures as the evil members of the life in the caverns continue to exist.

You who read may unwittingly meet one of the less hideous evil beings at any time on the surface. Those who come up from the caves for commercial or less honest reasons are, naturally, of the higher grades among them; for the degenerates are idiotic devils who only to be seen would be recognized as malevolence incarnate.

I will try to tell you something of them, for they everlastingly obstruct and bedevil mankind. It is their chief satisfaction to wreak pain and damage and death upon human beings. It is well to be able to recognize such enemies, for they are possessed of mighty weapons such as surface people have not yet conceived despite the many instruments of destruction fabricated for Earth wars. It is ghastly, but perhaps better for surface people in the final analysis, that these horrible beings have no actual brain power that can be used for intellectual pursuits or abstract theorizing; brain in them has been usurped by a continual questing for something to torment, to ray the life out of. They are like leeches in human form, wholly parasitic and destructive.

Merritt knew much of such things and gave it to you. I can add a great deal to what he has told you and I shall do so, nor shall any craven fear of the hidden powers stop me. For in those still existent mechanisms lie many infinitely valuable methods of making life bloom and become a vastly more beautiful and longer lasting thing than the present treadmill routine of war and work that it is.

I also address myself to those higher beings of the underworld, those who have kept the ancient virtues alive by breeding with stolen women from the surface, and for other reasons are well-intentioned and closer to mankind than the inbred degenerates peopling many of the caves. Such higher beings are as maliciously plagued as we by the idiot beings who hate everything that are noble and beautiful. The need of those kindlier beings for awareness of certain things, which

I have woven into my work, is as great as is the need of surface people for knowledge of their ancient enemies.

Merritt did not make quite clear the fact that the ancient weapons and mechanisms were, many of them, still intact in a great many places on earth. In confining his ancient, still living race to a hidden section of the Andes Mountains, he inadvertently concealed the general dispersion of these underground cities. Concealed in monstrous caverns of unbelievable breadth and space, these wondrous works of the ancient God-race are being used by the evil ones whom Merritt concepts as Nimir and Lantlu and his followers, but whom I picture more nearly to the facts of the case as degenerate men with a mind more in tune with such forms of life as a fluke or leech than to man. There are many such, protected from man on the surface by those hidden, inaccessible caverns whose walls are of such impenetrably hardened rock that the finest tools of miners are broken against them. On guard also at the few existent entrances are the ancient weapons whose great range render it impossible for any living thing to approach within a radius of thirty miles unless permitted by the watchers in the caves.

The power of Nimir's evil is not shackled as Merritt would have it in "The Face in the Abyss." On the contrary, it works havoc through its wretched dupes and hereditary morons, obstructing the good that the scattered Wise of the caverns would do for mankind; as well as blocking in subtle, long-practiced and undetected ways the progress of surface science. On both counts the reason for this mischief is not alone the hateful intent of these *dero*, but their fear lest surface science wakens to their existence and discovers some way of reaching them in the caverns and freeing the planet from their age-old deviltry.

It is a grievous thing to learn how much of beauty and ecstasy life can offer and yet be obliged to live on day after day in the wretched misery, which life in modern ways is to one who knows how the Ancients lived. In reading these tales, compare your life with the ancient ways one may learn in the caverns. You surface folk know nothing better than your present circumscribed existence, but I tell you that your lives are imprisoned hells from which modern science could free you overnight if your learned men would so overcome prejudices as to accept the fact of the existence of the ancient science and acquire but one piece of the marvelous mechanisms for study. And here let me add, for open, general study; not that secret abortive study that such ancient science has had in the past.

My strength is dedicated to informing you of the key and the way to the kind of life that produced the beauty and wisdom of those immortal beings of the past, beings whose actual existence has been proved a thousand times to those who, like myself, have had actual experience in the caverns. For we have seen and touched and used those antique mechanisms and we know whereof we speak. But until today, those who knew have feared to broadcast their knowledge, for in olden times it would have meant being burnt at the stake, and today most certainly the insane asylum.

Merritt well knew, as do I, that the Ancients had conquered death. I have set myself to tell you what I know of how they did so; and how plans carried out intelligently and with care can bring victory over death to modern surface men as it did to those Elders of long ago. It is not easy to achieve immortality, but a real start toward eventual success can be made.

I am forced to tell you that the work of such writers as Merritt contains much that is not fiction, but must be presented as fiction because no one would print it in any other form. Thus you readers who have not met the dark and unfathomable life of the hidden pits may take this bit of explanation as an effort to make an incredible story credible; in which case I hope the effort is successful. It is to those of you who either know, or who believe me, that I more significantly address myself.

Very sincerely yours,
Richard Shaver

This letter is an introduction to the story, which begins on the following page. As you read it, please bear in mind that it is presented to entertain you, and can be accepted as pure fiction, if you wish. But the fact remains, the author believes it is true—and your editor is as impressed as you will be!—Ed. (Raymond A. Palmer)

Introduction to
"Thought Records of Lemuria"
by Raymond A. Palmer

THE editors of this magazine are pleased to present the second "Lemurian" story written by a man who has seen with his own eyes the remnants of the ancient race of Lemuria, and witnessed their still-populated cities hidden deep beneath the surface of the Earth. This second story is intended to answer the challenge of those who wish Mr. Shaver to offer some proof of his source for the first story, "I Remember Lemuria!" published in our March issue. Although it is now revealed that Mr. Shaver's source is not racial memory, as mistakenly claimed by your editors, it seems certain that the actual source will be even more unbelievable. In the following pages you will find a story of amazing adventure, and thrills galore, in the true tradition of all science fiction—and yet, we ourselves cannot say that it is entirely fiction. It may even be that when the proofs now being produced are marshaled together, it will be discovered that a great deal of this and the first story (and stories to follow) are true in the most exact sense of the word. Meanwhile, we present this story for your enjoyment, and we welcome your comment. It is something NEW in science fiction!

Thought Records of Lemuria
—Originally edited by Raymond A. Palmer—

WHEN the blind girl of the caves turned on the thought record machine. I lived once more the life that was on Earth when the God races settled the planet, and learned their great scientific secrets.

"HEY, Joe Raddatz, bring that dolly over here!" I glanced up casually from my spot welding, then blinked in puzzlement as my eyes took in the area immediately around me. The voice in my ear had come out of nowhere! No fellow worker in this Detroit auto plant was near enough for his voice to be heard by me!

"What in the devil…" I muttered, then shrugged in mystification and turned back to my work.

The moment I snapped the switch on my spot welder the voice came again.

"…know damn well this rivet won't fit! Don't tell me I don't know a nine-thirty second hole when I see one…" The voice died away, and although I listened intently for a long moment, it didn't come again.

The noon whistle blew and I knocked off. But I didn't get much kick out of eating my lunch. I kept thinking about hearing that voice when no one was around me. Funny thing!

"Wonder who Joe Raddatz is?" I mumbled. I downed the last of my coffee and put the thermos bottle back in the lid of my lunch kit. Then I got to my feet, hitched up my trousers, and went down to the timekeeper's cubbyhole.

"Do me a favor, Clocky?" I asked.

"Sure thing," he grunted. "If it's anything I can do without getting off my fanny."

"It is. I just want to know if there's a Joe Raddatz working on this shift, and where he's located."

Clocky twisted around on his high stool, faced an index on the wall, and ran one finger down the row of cards that were inserted in little slots. "Raddatz—? Uh—yeah, here it is. Sure, Joe Raddatz is on this shift. Works over in section twenty. That'd be down at the far end of the building—he's a riveter."

"Thanks, Clocky," I said, and walked back toward my section. I was frowning and the information I'd just heard was revolving in my brain like a silly pinwheel, getting nowhere.

"Section twenty—" I mumbled, stumbling over a barrel of bronze welding rods. "How could I hear a guy talking over there?"

I thought of acoustics, and pursed my lips. "Yeah, maybe I could, at that." They say there's a spot in the old senate chambers in the Capitol Building where even the faintest whisper can be heard from a spot ninety feet away, and most peculiarly, can be heard at no other point. Acoustics are a funny thing—just the way a building is built can carry sounds and direct them to points where they couldn't ordinarily be heard. Some caves are like that; you can hear a voice a mile away, when it would be inaudible otherwise at a hundred feet.

Thinking about it that way took all the mystery out of it, and I grinned. "Takes a mighty little thing to make a guy think he's dopey!" I said aloud.

I reached my bench and sat down to wait for the whistle to begin work again. By the time it blew I forgot all about Joe Raddatz and acoustics.

AT TWO o'clock the voice came again. This time it wasn't the voice of Joe Raddatz. It was a new voice, hoarse and gruff; and there were only two words he seemed to be able to fit together coherently. They aren't the kind I'd ordinarily repeat. A moment later I heard other voices—

voices of men all up and down the plant, and after an hour I had learned two things: all of the voices came from the side of the plant on which I worked, from one end to the other. I couldn't hear them when I laid my welding gun down. Somehow the two facts were connected.

By nightfall I had figured it out; the voices of the men were those who were near, or in contact with, some machine attached to the wiring system on my side of the building. I couldn't hear any voices at all as long as I didn't have any physical contact with my spot welder.

I think I breathed easier. After all, there was an explanation that I was perfectly willing and able to accept. The wire system, and the machines connected to it, was somehow acting in a telephonic manner, picking up voices, transmitting them through the electrical circuit, and reproducing them in my gun. When I turned the thing in that evening I spoke to the stockroom supervisor.

"Pete, how about sending this in for a repair job—it's out of order."

"What's wrong with it?"

"Gives me a shock," I lied. I figured it was better to say that than go through the rigmarole that would be necessary to explain how I heard voices through it; and the possibility existed that he'd snort and say I was nuts, and I wouldn't get a new gun—and I wanted one. It's nerve-wracking to have to act like a telephone receiver when you're supposed to concentrate on your work.

A new spot welder didn't do any good. The next day I heard the voices again.

There was only one thing to do—I stuffed my ears with cotton.

And I still heard them!

NOW I began to get a little scared. I wasn't *hearing* these voices; I was *thinking* them! They were in my mind, soundless, inaudible. Mental telepathy!

Men about me, near or far, saying things, *thinking* things, and I could hear every spoken word or every most secret thought.

I knew I was receiving the thoughts of some of these men, because, for instance, I heard: "Sure, Mike, you're right about that…*Right! If this guy's right, I'll eat his shirt!…*you're the boss, we'll do it your way…*and nuts to you. After you're down the line I'll do as I damned please! For a foreman, you're the stupidest—*" No workman would talk to his foreman like that.

I heard other things that were more convincing proof that I was hearing thoughts, things that made me blush when I heard them; and I don't blush easy!

Right now, for instance, a guy is thinking about his girl… Say, if she thinks he loves her, somebody ought to put her straight! He's a wrong guy, but really I ought to tip her off—

Hey, wait a minute, how would I *prove* the truth of my tip?

Dynamite that's what this is! I'll have to keep my trap shut, or I'll be putting my foot into it. I never realized how bad it might be to know what the other guy is thinking, without him being aware you know.

"Put him on the rack," said a voice.

I snapped off my welder and sat still, frowning. Something was wrong with that voice, or thought, or whatever it was. Put him on the rack? You don't put people on a rack in an auto plant. Tools, yes, or a lot of other things. Rack? What sort of a rack?

"It'll pull him apart in an hour!" the voice went on with a note of horrible satisfaction in it. "Nice and slow, so he suffers plenty! Put the ben ray on him, so he won't die too quick…"

My welding gun clattered to the cement floor. I stood as though frozen. The hair on my head crawled. What was I hearing?

The voice was gone. All around me was only the muted roar of an auto factory—the clanging, clattering, mingling maelstrom of busy machines and busier men. Just noise, no voices.

I LOOKED down at the gun on the floor and I was trembling. What was going on? That voice had been no voice, or thought, of a worker in this plant...unless it was the thought of a madman!

A madman?

I sat down, white and shaken as the thought struck me. Maybe *I* was mad! Maybe there were no voices at all. Maybe I'd never actually heard the voices of anyone else. Maybe my own mind was cracking up, and inflicting these weird illusions upon me.

But no. After all, there was Joe Raddatz. I had the name okay, and he actually worked here. And there were other men in the plant whom I'd identified since. Somehow I *had* heard voices, and real thoughts.

Or was *that* insanity? Did insane people go insane simply because their brain functioned *too well?* Is an insane person only a person whose brain is more active than it should be? Is he using that nine tenths of his brain that science says is just dormant and waiting for his future evolution into a higher type of creature? Just what *is* insanity, after all?

They put people who hear voices into nut houses. But maybe they *do* hear the voices. Maybe they aren't insane at all. Maybe they are just like me!

I looked at the gun again. A thought struck me. If I'm nuts, then I'd be nuts without the gun in my hands. I'd hear these voices any time; maybe all the time. Pick up the gun and see—

I picked up the gun and watched it shake from the trembling of my hands—

The horrible scream of agony that echoed in my brain jolted me right up to my feet with a gasp, and with a cry of terror I hurled the gun from me and ran. Through my mind echoed that scream of utter pain, the scream of a human being in such torture as might be imagined only in Dante's Inferno. Somewhere, somehow, a human being was dying in slow agony—*and I was hearing him die!*

I couldn't stand any more. I managed to slow to a rapid walk, but I kept on going until I got to Clocky's cage.

"Punch in my time, Clocky," I gasped. "I'm quitting. I've had enough of—of welding," I finished weakly.

Clocky stared at me peculiarly, then grunted, punched my card and handed it to me.

"You can get your check at the office," he said gruffly. "Sorry to see you go, Dick." He looked at me queerly. "Say, you ain't sick, are you?"

"No—no!" I said hastily. "I'm okay. Just decided I don't like welding. Besides, I want to take a vacation for awhile. I've been working too hard, maybe. Guess that's why you think I look sick…"

I mumbled the last words as I walked away. I didn't look back. Why should I? One thing was sure. I had seen the last I was going to see of that damned welding gun! If I wasn't nuts, that gun would make me so sooner or later.

A HALF-hour later I was out of the plant on a streetcar heading for home.

"His hotel's clear through," said a voice. "He dug up a lot of stuff and he's getting too smart."

I, Richard Shaver, was going insane, I was sure of it now! I sat there in that street car with the awfulest feeling of fear I have ever experienced, listening to the absolutely crazy babblings of my own mind. How could it be anything else? Even if this were mental telepathy, how could I tie up such a phenomenon with the things I heard? They didn't make sense. Even insane people make sense, but this last voice in my mind—*his hotel's clear through*—what does that mean?

"He's dug the cellar of his house clear down to the caves," the voice explained.

The voice in my mind had answered my question! I sat as though I'd been struck by lightning. But I still had some sense left in my head—I gasped out another question, this time audibly and the man next to me turned to stare at me blankly. "How deep is that?" was what I said.

"About three hundred feet—" said the voice, and suddenly there was a startled note in it, and it faded away. At the same time I felt a numbing shock in my neck, in my spinal column, and I almost screamed with agony from the blinding headache that sprang into being.

"Say, mister," said the man next to me, "you'd better get home and to bed—you look sick!"

I stared at him through pain-filled eyes. "Yeah," I gasped. "I had better. I am sick… Got a terrible headache." I climbed to my feet and staggered to the rear of the car and got off.

I walked the rest of the way to my room, fighting the blinding pain in my head. I barely made it to my bed before I blacked out. And as I blacked out I knew a faint glimmering of the truth. Somehow, by some weird super-scientific means, unseen beings had caused this headache—possibly the same ones I'd heard talking that weird gibberish about the hotel—and that I'd brought it upon myself by asking questions. I'd revealed the fact that I had been listening in, and it hadn't been a welcome discovery. The pain-filled blackness into which I sank now was proof of that.*

WHEN I awoke my headache was gone, but not my fear. I fled from Detroit as though the devil himself were after me.

To no avail; I could not escape the voices. I heard them day after day, night after night. It went on for months until finally I had become more or less accustomed to them—until I began to understand the whole horrible picture. And also came to understand the fate that was in store for me.

The voices came from beings I came to realize were not human; not normal modern men at all. They lived in great caves far beneath the surface. These alien minds I listened to seemed to know that they had great power, seemed conscious of the fact that they were evil. However they also seemed to think themselves infinitely clever, but the truth of the matter was that they were obviously stupid. I discovered this from

---

*As dramatically as it is possible for me to do so, I have pictured those first weird happenings that led me almost to the brink of madness, and then to the most incredible adventure that ever befell a man. In order to give my knowledge to the world without being suspected of madness, I must present it in the guise of fiction. Remember that all this wordiness is supposed to be, but is not, just a way of convincing you momentarily of the truth of an obvious impossibility, for the sake of the escape from dull reality, which it offers you. So allow yourself really to believe, not just temporarily for the sake of the effect. This story will not seem like fiction to some who will read it. For it is substantially true; the caves, the good and wise users of the antique machines, the fantastic evil mis-users of the antique weapons, all these things are true things and exist in secret in many parts of the world.

Keeping that secret has been a custom, a hereditary habit of the Elder underworld. Surface incredulity and fear of the supernatural has made it an open secret that keeps itself; for you will find that the case records of insane asylums are chock full of patients whose only complaint was that they heard mysterious voices in their minds.

In this story, I intend to reveal the secret to the world, to those who have the intelligence to seek to understand what I say.—Author.

listening very, very carefully. Their thoughts were incredibly contradictory, to make things worse was to get along better, to make enemies was to be more powerful, to torment anyone was a personal satisfaction, to love any living thing was weak and stupid.

Who were these voices? Where were they? It took me several years to figure it out, but finally I was successful. And when I finally had learned the truth, they knew that I had discovered it, was becoming informed as to them, their place of residence, their mode of living, their evil thoughts. And since fear is one of their mainsprings, they feared me.

It was not too long before I could overhear them in my mind, plotting my destruction, though why they should have had any trouble about that I could not at that time understand. When I gained more knowledge of their stupid, crazy minds' workings, and learned that they believed they cannot actually kill a surface man without first building up a frame for the killing that will make it appear either suicide or accident or death from natural causes, I began to realize what was ahead of me.

This belief of theirs is based primarily upon their fear of discovery and its implications, plus a more realistic danger: though often stupid and usually duped, there exist among these *dero** people many who are not as malicious and evil as

----

*This is a shortening of the term "detrimental robot." It means, briefly, that they are "people who are slaves to a degenerate mind." Their brains have become radioactively poisoned by rays from the weird machines they constantly use and whose use they do not fully understand and whose rays become detrimental because of non-replacement of vital parts, which thus becomes impregnated with radioactive accumulations whose emanations are harmful (just as radium must be shielded by lead to prevent serious burns). Thus all their thinking is along destructive channels. Obviously, then, a "tero" (in contrast to a "dero") is one whose thinking is integrative, or constructive, in quality because his mind has not been poisoned by radioactives.—Ed.

the worst degenerates, and these *tero* are impelled to avenge murder committed for no really good reason, even when it is the murder of one of the helpless, because unknowing, surface people.

"He knows too much; we must kill him," became a frequent thought I heard in their minds, and it terrified me. I tried desperately to contact the only ones I knew could help me, the *tero*, but I did not succeed. I was neatly framed, and here is how they did it:

They framed me subtly and completely, so subtly that I myself, although aware from hearing their thoughts what they were up to, did not realize how to avoid the trap until it was too late. I fell for every one of their tricks, because their devious deviltry and their incomprehensibly stupid motivations were not yet clarified in my mind. It was under their control that I did a thing that proved to their enemies, the *tero*, (whose vengeance they feared and whose conscience they had to find a means of dulling by building up a case sufficiently plausible to deceive them into accepting my fate as necessary) that I was no friend.

After that came the harpy hue and cry, which has for ages followed and caused the death of the best minds among surface men from persecution by their own kind. Daily it rang in my ears while I fled from city to city to escape it. Yet, when my brother became involved and they killed him, I argued with myself that I must be having delusions that his death was natural, that all this could not be without some mention of it in the papers or in books.

I SHALL not take more of your time to give the details of how the axe fell on me; it is all too sordid. I assure you it did not do me credit, and I would much rather forget it. Suffice it to say that my enforced escapade, which I was blindly urged into by the subtle energy of the telepathy machines and other incomprehensible mechanisms using rays and forces that surface man never heard of, ended with my arrest and sentence to a state prison.

To this end those potent rays in the hands of evil idiots had driven me, a well-intentioned human being, in earth's hidden caverns!

But that I was thus imprisoned was not enough. They poured continuously upon me pain rays that, added to mental control which continually got me into disgusting, dangerous situations, kept me on the verge of madness from despair for years. I learned at length and in infinite detail just what Hell really can be, and at the same time I realized that such a Hell has been the daily lot of many men of Earth since earliest times.

There was no relief or way of seeking aid from the continuous and almost unbearable torment. And had I complained to a prison guard that I was being tormented by invisible rays, I would have been taken from the prison to be shut up in a madhouse. I knew there would then be no hope of release. Waiting and patience might at length gain my release here at the end of my sentence; but in a madhouse, once certified mad by medical men, I realized that I would not even have the solace of attempted flight from the *dero* rays, to the end of my days. For from the talk of other prisoners I knew a madhouse to be a much harder place to get out of than a prison.

I know those *dero* only let me live because my life was a burden to me, and because my torture was a delight to them and they feared no retribution.

I had become but a thin, haggard ghost of a man when release came from a quarter I had lost all hope of ever contacting. In some manner the *tero*, the sane, well meaning members of that strange cavern life, seized control of the area of land in which the prison lay.

MY TORMENTS ceased abruptly. A new and intensely wonderful life began for me. For the first time in years I was able to relax, although for some time I lived in dread of the return of the suffering to which I had grown almost accustomed, as one grows accustomed to a painful limp.

I began to dream and my dreams were infinitely pleasant though bizarre in the extreme. I could not recall them wholly upon awaking until one night *she* came to me in my dream, and that dream was as fresh in my memory when I wakened as though it had been an actual reality. She came to my cell, apparently, and sat herself upon the edge of my iron cot. With her came that laughing spirit of youth and mischievousness, which I had almost forgotten as the face of freedom. The oppressive feeling that is a part of prison life vanished; she had brought her free face before my eyes.

She seemed clothed in a soft luminosity that threw rays of strangely invigorating light upon me as well as showing her strange, rich otherworld beauty to me. She had hair of faintest golden tint, just off white, and it lay smoothly drawn back from her brow and was caught at the nape of her neck with a ribbon that was a pale green, a green that had lain so long in darkness that it had lost its original color. Her eyes under arching brows were wide and had no expression, yet her assurance in every movement as she came into the cell did not betray what I learned later, that she was blind. The eyes were very large, and faintly blue. Her features were not out of the ordinary, but strangely and beautifully exaggerated: the too-large eyes; the delicate, utterly sensitive nose; the drooping, too-large lips that were made for caresses they had not received. Her beauty was far from the standard variety one finds under the surface sun. She had that strange, wise quality men have sung of as the witch maid's alone since time began. When she spoke, such vitality sprang into being on her strange face as woke every instinct in me from the long hopeless sleep in which they had been plunged. Yes, her face was freedom to me.

She wore a loose garment that hung from her shoulders to her calves and was belted by a metal circlet of netted links into which was thrust a metallic object which I recognized as a weapon of some strange kind.

IN MY dream I sat upright. My youthful visitor took both my hands in hers, saying—

"Do you wish freedom so badly, then?"

I replied: "I want it more than life, but capture would be inevitable. Then I would get no more chances to escape."

"If you are willing," her halting, apparently little used English voice said, "I can take you to a place where no police have ever shown their face, and where none ever will. You have only to agree to do as I tell you, without argument, for one year. I can free you quickly, and in truth I need your services."

I embraced with enthusiasm any prospect of escape, and could not imagine that "doing her bidding" would be anything but pleasant. I agreed to her proposition, adding some fervent prayers of confused and stumbling words that I hoped expressed my infinite despair and the bright face of the hope she brought me.

Thus came to me Nydia, as I called the blind girl after the blind maiden in Bulwer Lytton's "Fall of Pompeii." In the morning after that first dream of her I found upon the cot that pale ribbon she had worn about her paler hair. I knew then that it was more than a dream and I looked forward with mounting anticipation to further meetings with a person who could come to a man as a dream and leave behind an actual memento. How had that ribbon gotten through those walls and bars?

It was some time before the magic was explained to me. She had promised me that she would very soon find means to release me from the prison, and that mysteriously actual ribbon was a constant reminder in my pocket that she had powers beyond present day wisdom. I still do not understand how those antique teleport mech's* work, but work they do, and she had sent the ribbon over it after she had shut off the dream-maker machine. But I will explain that later.

After that, she came to me frequently, sometimes she was just a kind of projection, and sometimes her sweet, actual body lay in my arms, I swear. I grew accustomed to her visits and the hopes I began to entertain built me up more and more in morale, particularly as I was no longer tormented. In time I realized that she loved me truly, a man who had not seen a woman in many years of imprisonment. She loved me in dreams more vivid than any reality could be, made so by the stronger-than-human thought impulses sent over her strange dream-making instrument's rays.

She loved me with the first maiden love of a girl for a man, for she herself had long been a prisoner in one of the caves and was but now set free. She read in my heart all that I was, and our mutual and long desire for freedom that becomes a constant part of one's thoughts after long imprisonment brought about between us a kinship that blossomed swiftly into glowing love for each other. So it was not long before she told me all was ready, that she would come that very night during the darkness before dawn, to free

----

*Teleport mech—a means of transmission over a distance of an actual object by means of tele rays. This machine could transmit a solid thing in a way that might be comparable to the way a photo or map is transmitted by radio. However, there is a difference in principle, which Mr. Shaver has never been able to fathom from his study of the machine.—Ed.

me, and to take me with her into her hidden home.

THAT same night the key grated in the lock of my cell door and I was not surprised to see the guard standing there as if dazed, his eyes unseeing. By then I understood something of her powers, and understood that he was a man under mental control. Behind him I could see reproduced the form of the blind girl, her transparent form bending over a huge old mechanism, her face a mask of concentration. The guard waited until I had emerged, almost cringing in my dread lest this was just another dream from which I might awaken, then he locked the cell door behind me, the cell now empty of its victim. We walked to the outer door that led from the corridor. This he opened and stood waiting to lock it again after I had passed out. I looked at him curiously, for his face was peaceful as in sleep and his eyes were unseeingly fixed ahead on space.

Silently as a shadow I slid out and no sound ever was so sweet as that door's lock clicking shut behind me. I sped across the open grounds and into the nearby forest and there beside me again was that transparent slim ghost of Nydia leading me by the hand. To my undying amazement, the projection of that miraculous ancient mechanism felt as solid to my hand as real human flesh, though very different and thrilling because of the augmentative nature of the mechanism. Love with augmentation is immensely more desirable than normal love.

For miles that phantasm led me deeper and deeper into the hills. In the dark I could visualize every stone and bit of dead branch as though my feet had eyes of their own. They did—a blind girl's electric perception, developed since she was a child in the use of those miraculously potent and indestructible mechanisms, was able to sense those trifling obstacles and lead me clearly among them.

As last we came to the base of the mountain, to where it reared rocky slopes to the night sky. In the cleft of two rocky shoulders yawned a door. It was a strange door, for it was covered with earth and grass and small bushes, all alive and growing. As soon as our feet crossed the threshold, the great mass of the door lowered silently and I knew that no man could detect where that door might be.*

THE dim light inside the cave I found emanated from long tubes running along the walls, which contained some self-actuating material, which glows. Once, it was probably productive of a strong light, but now it gave off but a dim glow. The blind girl sensed my thoughts and spoke: "In other of the caverns there is brilliant light which can be switched on and off. There the tubes are wired to one of the ancient dynamos, which must now and then be replenished by water, which is the fuel of many of the ancient power generators.* In those caves, the dwellers have normal eyesight."

Into this twilight the ghostly little figure continued to draw me on. We emerged at length into a vast room, around which could be dimly seen huge mechanisms of incomprehensible uses. Beside one of these stood a soft, utterly enticing figure that was the duplicate of the phantasm

---

*Such doors into the caves are few but they do exist and no other door is so worthy of a man's search. Always provided the door is not one that opens upon the hiding places of the evil life that is in many parts of the caves, there is no door that can open life before you as that door to the underworld. Read on and you shall learn something of the pleasure and wisdom that opened door offered me, a criminal escaped from a state prison. You shall learn, too, that there are other things yet more wonderful than the seemingly impossible feat of a blind girl snatching a convict out of a prison.—Author.

---

*The water is disintegrated by some unknown process.—Ed.

that had led me here. The screen still glowed brightly from use. As my footsteps rang on the ancient polished stone of the floor, this little figure raced toward me unerringly and threw herself into my arms. Her no-longer dropping, flower-red mouth sought mine like a starved animal scenting meat. As she left the receptor screen of the ancient mechanism, the phantom beside me disappeared abruptly.

"Dick, my poor love! You are safe with me at last. It has seemed so long," cried her voice that was music to me who had starved for the tender tones of a woman's voice for so many years.

My arms went about her slender child's form. I leaned my face to those questing lips and learned more about love in two seconds than all the past of my life had taught me. The little witch had left the augmentor beam on me and only those who have loved under those ancient impulse augmentors can understand the depths of love. I knew that I had never really lived until that fierce moment when our love sprang into flaming life.

At last we stood, just looking at each other. I felt sure that Nydia could see me, her intent wide eyes were fixed so surely on me.

"I cannot believe that you do not actually see me!" I exclaimed.

"Almost I do," she responded. "You seem much bigger, now that you are here. My mind can see you, in a way that you will learn to see, too."

I looked about for the first time. I realized that my little sweetheart was but poorly clad, not at all like the projection she had made of herself into my prison cell. I learned later that that projection was largely mental, so that her likeness went clad as she would have liked to be clothed. In reality her garments were but a few well-worn rags. I myself could have wished I wore less than my prison denim, for the temperature was high, as it is in deep mines. Her fair hair, her large unseeing eyes, her paper white skin, were as I had seen them in my prison.

The vast round space where we stood was surrounded by hulking, mysterious machines; they stood dimly gigantic in the faint light of the cavern lamps.

I ASKED Nydia where her people were. She said with a little laugh that they were leaving us to ourselves at this moment of our meeting but that I should meet them soon enough.

"Oh, Dick, in some ways they are different from surface folk, and you must not let these differences disturb you. They are prepared to welcome you heartily because I love you and they love me. But it is not our custom to admit surface people to our hidden ways, for they are so apt to fear us and thus hate and be a danger to us. Greet them naturally and show no fear or repulsion no matter how they look to you. We are different from the kind of human you are used to. We need men like you to aid us in our constant struggle with the living devils that inhabit much of these underground warrens. But when we try to approach men for this purpose they fear the whole thing as madness or ghosts or whatever they have been taught. You see, we are forced to fight the devils because we wish evil to no one and cannot be glad when others suffer, and that is a way of thought that all the evil cavern wights* hate and seek to destroy."

She led me from the huge machinery cavern into a smaller room that was a strange mixture of architectural magnificence, the work of the Gods, and old hand-made wooden furniture that must have been brought into that place two hundred years ago, or more. We sat on a wooden bench that was a half of an oak tree, split length-wise, with wooden

----

*Wight—an elf. In this case, the *dero* people.—Ed.

pegs for legs. She told me more of her people. They had come from England's northern underground seventy years before. They were but few, only twenty living in the ruined splendor of that ancient God's retreat. Most of them had never read a book, although Nydia had a few poor samples of modern books. But they had read men's minds over the ancient beams that penetrated through miles of the rock of the hills and was so conductive and augmentive one could read a man's mind many miles away. In some ways they knew more of life than does the ordinary man by far.

Many of them had contacted surface folk and striven to persuade such persons to join them but had been rebuffed probably from a fear that their soft invitation was a mental delusion or masked some snare. For those men who know of the ancient secret know also of the evil it has always done, hence fear all ray people* though many are wise and good and try to nullify the evil and reduce the torments inflicted by the degenerate evil members of that strange life.

OF THE twenty in this group at least a half-dozen were blind because of their heredity, like Nydia. For many of the

---

*Ray people are taken to mean all of the modern underground race, both the dero and the tero. They are called "ray" by Mr. Shaver because that is the means they use to spy upon surface people, and to talk to them, and to perform the many weird things their machines are capable of doing. It is by rays that they operate. For instance, have you ever had a fearful nightmare in which you have been faced by horribly realistic monstrosities such as your waking mind has never conceived, to your utter terror? This dream might have been produced in your mind by tele-projection from the dero creatures of the caves who delight in causing surface people horror and terror. There is another and more significant reason behind this practice, and that is to build up superstition and fear in surface people that has been proved their greatest protection against discovery by upper-worlders. They fear discovery because it would mean their extermination by a vindictive human race, seeking to revenge itself upon its age-old torturers.—Ed.

cavern people come of stock that lived so long in almost total darkness as to become blind as the fish in cavern rivers become blind. Ages of life in the dark had developed other senses than sight in their particular family, compensatory senses. The others, strangely enough, had very large eyes, much too large for normal vision, with great black openings in the iris. Evolution had developed the faculty of seeing in the dark in these. Their skins were often light brown; or a paper-like, bleached white; or a mottled, strangely lumpy appearance, which came of a disease peculiar to the caves. They are not like surface men, these dwellers in the caves.

But these *tero* were a kindly lot and a friend of Nydia's was a friend of theirs. I soon saw that they had little comprehension of the terrific significance of the ancient secret of the caverns' mechanisms or the value of a knowledge of their uses. It was difficult to realize their lack of imagination and their casual acceptance of the facts of their age-old customs in regard to surface men. It is not, after all, so many years ago when all such people were burned as witches and sorcerers. They had never attended a school, yet their knowledge in general was surprising for people raised in practically total darkness. It is because they absorb general information from reading many men's minds. The fact that rickets is not common among them I attribute to the beneficial rays, which the ancients made a part of the pleasure-ray machines, which they are proficient in using from long practice.

Perhaps our education and its consequent results in thought are not as important or remarkable, as we of the surface believe. Certainly our thoughts offer these *tero* small temptation to join us; they prefer, I think wisely, their seclusion. Nydia, not alone among her kind, but rare, had vast plans and different ideas than theirs; she had always urged contact with surface people and had at last fallen in love with a surface man and brought him with her into her cavern home.

THE space within the mountain was an Aladdin's cave, beautiful beyond a modern man's imagination. The hall where Nydia next led me, saying it was a hall where the group met for any social purposes, was pillared by mighty metal simulations of trees, hung with crystalline, glittering fruits. In every one of these great rooms stood several of the enigmatic ancient mechanisms, themselves beautiful of form and shimmering with prismatic color.

Some of the machines had a startling way of talking; when one neared them they would speak in a strange tongue, beautiful sounding words of a meaning incomprehensible. That is a strange sensation, hearing a machine speak to you. I suspect they were equipped to announce their need of oil or other minor adjustments, as we equip mechanisms with red lights to indicate need for adjustment.

The solid, gleamingly polished and super-hard floor of rock was inlaid with weirdly beautiful designs and symbols, which I deduced were writings in the Ancient's lost language. Imperishable metal lounges, once probably covered with the "shining fabrics which the Gods alone could weave"* stood beside the gleaming, ancient "mech," as the cavern people call the old machines. It was in this great room that later that same night, or day, I should perhaps say, Nydia's family and other members of that group formally welcomed me, the surface man who had joined them for the balance of his life.

AMONG the cavern people, marriage is purely a personal matter, they either live together or they do not, it is no one else's business. I often think their attitude in this respect is

----

*"Shining fabrics which the Gods alone can weave" is verbatim from "Ulysses."—Ed.

the correct one. In the caves, when two people promise themselves to each other, they keep their promise; which is more than I can say for surface life. Nydia spent exactly one week showing me that what happened to Tannhauser in the Hollow Hill with the goddess Venus can still happen to mortal man. She had studied the uses of the antique pleasure mechanisms under masters—some of whom I met later. For one week I experienced all the pleasures of a God's nuptials; tremendous stimulation generators poured super-powered pleasure impulses through every nerve of my body at their full capacity. If a man could die of pleasure I am sure that I would have died then. But my tender hearted Nydia was no slave of pleasure. She was a sweet normal girl in love and I learned more of what infinite pleasure life could hold in that week than ever mortal man did before.

At the week's end, my little blind witch began to talk of other things than love and of honeymooning. I will admit that I protested at length, but she gave me her reasons quietly but firmly.

"There is much you must learn, my innocent, if you would live very long down here. We may at any time be attacked by savage, mad ray-men from the evil places. You do not yet know how to fight or work with these tremendous weapons. We cannot wait. Besides you have promised to do as I say for one year, and my purpose in making you promise this to me was just that, that I might teach you to be of value to us in such a fight."

"I am yours and you may do with me as you please," I told her gravely, and I meant it.

"I shall show you, dear lover, the true nature of those whom we must fight against if we are to survive," she said, musingly. "There is so much to tell you, to teach you, that I hardly know where to begin. But first of all you must know whom it is that we must battle against. Come!"

She led me to the great hall where I had first met her and paused before one of the mechanisms. Her hand on the control, she swung a huge distance-ray beam and almost immediately upon the visi-screen a scene of utter horror became visible. I could hardly believe my own eyes' evidence. That was a Hell, a real Hell, I looked upon. Men hung swinging from hooks, boiled in fluids, writhed on racks, thirsted in the stocks, sat on spikes tugging to get off, lay under hammers that crushed them inch by slow inch, or slid inexorably into machines that sliced them gradually with the thinness of a microtome.*

NYDIA explained the horror, and I got at last the full significance of the ancient legend of Hell.

"You see, they will not allow their victims to die, but keep them alive through every torment by the use of the beneficial rays. When a man is nearly dead, they place him in one of the vitalizer machines for a day or two and he is healed up completely. Then they start him through the thing again. Do you see those shriveled bundles at the side? That is how the victims look when they finally do die."

We watched the horror for a space of time and Nydia concluded—

"Some of those men have lived in that torment for twenty years. This is our enemy's pleasure palace; a Hell for helpless victims of their lust for blood and pain. From immemorial times, they have had such Hells in the underworld, and it has never ceased. You see, you surface Christians are not so far wrong in your pictures of Hell, except that you do not die in order to go there, but wish for death to release you once you arrive. And they are very careful about letting a victim die, for that would end the fun. There has always been a Hell on

----

*One of various instruments used to cut sections for microscopic examination.—Ed.

Earth, and this is one of them. Every man who falls into their hands, from the caverns or from the surface, faces one of those torments-to-the-death you witness. It never mentions such things, your newspaper, does it? That bunch of misbegotten spawn of an afreet* fears all living men."

"Do any surface men know of this thing?" I asked her.

"It's impossible to tell them of such things," she answered. "Since there is no logical reason for anyone behaving as they do, none of the motives that animate surface people being evident in such activity, they can't believe any tale of modern Hell. Even if you show them projections of the things that go on in the evil caverns, they are sure that it is a concoction made up to frighten them, from motives wholly mischievous. The truth is, almost none of the surface people believe in the existence of evil ray-groups from antiquity down to the present day. They don't even understand the detrimental robotism* which is the underlying cause of such a horror.

And there is no way to tell them, short of taking them there. Even if they knew, what could they do? They have no weapons to fight an ancient ray weapon, nothing they could

----

*A monstrous evil jinni, a demon, a horrible giant.—Ed.

----

*Detrimental robotism—actually the two words from which dero is derived, using the first two letters of each word. Thus it can be seen that a dero is a being who is a robot (or slave) to a detrimental process of thinking, a process that always ends in something bad. Dero people's minds are affected, so that their thought processes are warped into evil channels. Picture the brain as poisoned, and picture a thought as something that must make its way through the convolutions. This is not actually what happens, but it is an analogy that will help you to understand. Conceive of the thought as a good thought, such as doing a good deed. But by the time the thought has gone through the brain and transmitted into action, the thought is no longer a good deed, but a bad deed. For instance you are impelled by your thought to help a blind man across the street, but by the time you get to him to do it, your thought has changed so that you trip him and laugh as he falls into a mud puddle. That is the way a dero thinks, and why he always does evil things—his brain is so poisoned by detrimental energy that all his good thoughts end up bad. Pure thought, say the philosophers, is always good. It is only rendered bad by the effect of a sick human mind.—Ed.

do would stop the thing. Since most of the victims come from among us cavern people, surface people never miss anyone without having a simple explanation for the disappearance."

SHE twirled a dial on the great apparatus and swiftly the picture on the screen swept through the beautiful caves and came to rest on a group of things that should not live.

"Do you see them?" she demanded. "Those things that could not live but for the beneficial rays they bathe in perpetually? The worst thing about them is their fear of technical men. They are so stupid they think that modern science might produce weapons affective against their mighty antique mechanisms, so they particularly persecute and obstruct modern scientists on the surface, although the truth is, it is improbable that men can produce anything equal to the ancient work in even centuries of effort."

"Have you had many other surface people here?" I asked her in wonder.

Nydia shook a sad little blonde head. "It is very difficult," she admitted.

"I have planned for years on recruiting and training a group of men who would be far superior in ability to those evil ones we fear. But surface men fear us, chiefly because they have heard the whispered lies and horrible thoughts of the evil ray-men."

I looked with loathing and sick disgust at the Things that were now pictured on the vast visi-screen. In truth, they could not have lived save for the protection and beneficial force rays of that Elder Race that had once lived there. Small wizened imps, goggle-eyed, their goblin appearance was that of walking dead men. And dead they would have been except for the synthetic body electric, which the ancient generators of life force pour through their bodies forever. Because of this supply of super energy, these evil people live on long after they would normally be dead. It is this fact, also, that makes them evil, for they are in truth not able to create thought, and only the slow decay of their brains is energized by the synthetic electric, which is the real cause of the evil, destructive nature of their thought. It is not genuine thought at all, but a reflection of the decay in their minds, which is a disintegrant pattern, not a creative one.

Nydia explained all this to me very clearly, and I know she was right, for they looked extremely unburied, long dead, but horribly alive. I believe that if they were cut off from this ancient supply of life-generating electric mechanisms, they would not live a week. Some of them hung over balconies around the scene of that hell upon which I had looked sickly a moment before. They were obviously gloating evilly. Others were talking over the telepathic ray mechanism with people on the surface.

"To torment their victims is their greatest pleasure. They have little ability to enjoy other things. And they are always amusing themselves torturing helpless beings that have fallen into their hands. It is a terrible thing to understand, but it is true."

"WHERE did this particular group come from?" I asked Nydia.

"The ancestors of this group came from underneath Arabia. They came long before we did, more than one hundred and fifty years ago. Some of them are one hundred and fifty years old, too, I have learned. The Arabs knew them as afreets, the devils that whisper in sand blowing at night, or scream like lost souls in the sand storms, and mislead the poor Arabs, causing their death with lies or tormenting them with pain rays."

But those afreets, or goblins, upon which I stared on the visi-screen were not whispering in the wind or the sand. They were, instead, lisping into the straining ears of some of the most influential tycoons of the surrounding surface industrial area. The lies they told! I learned later by myself, reading the minds of some of the rich, that many of them believed in the power and efficiency of the Secret Ray of America, which they thought was a service like the F.B.I. for the purpose of searching out escaped convicts, bank-robbers, extortioners, kidnapers, etc. To these tycoons the ray-dero from the hidden caverns posed as a secret service, hard at work solving several murders and robberies they had committed themselves. They were amazing mimics, considering that they had little real intelligence, but only a pseudo-thought arising from their long experience in reading men's minds.

"My dearest Dick, you must learn very quickly all that I can teach you," murmured Nydia tensely. "Then you will be better able to help our sane group—who are really very good and wise—protect ourselves from those mad ones. At present we are able to hold them off, but at any time they may get the better of us. They are really mad idiots, in spite of their clever mimicry of sane people's actions. They slay us whenever they have an opportunity to do so without loss or danger to themselves.

"Come, now!" Nydia continued, "—into the ancient thought record library. You shall read the history of the great race who builded these imperishable caves and the indestructible machinery which is capable of who knows what miracles. These records tell of a time when the Great Ones lived on Earth long before history was recorded by writing. Thus, you shall know more about the Earth and the life of Man in the past than any other living man from the surface— more, too, than most of the cavern people, for few of us study long enough to learn to appreciate and absorb the wisdom that lies in such places as this library of the recorded thought of the mighty men who were once called Gods by people of earth. This is the place that has made me intelligent and worthy of life. You will become a great man if you use this wisdom, my lover."

Into yet another chamber Nydia led me and guided me to a huge chair, like a giant's dentist chair, though the upholstery was missing. She pushed me into it, and I was lost in its tremendous size, which made her laugh deliciously. There were several flexible metal straps, which she fastened about my wrists, waist and neck. Then she took a strange helmet, fastened to a heavy cable, and placed it on my head.*

"Lie back and relax. You will soon be another person entirely in another period of time. Do not let the double sensation of

----

*When I gave the world the story of Mutan Mion (In "I Remember Lemuria!" in the March, 1945, AMAZING STORIES) as my own memories, I could not reveal exactly how I remembered the far past, without bringing the story down to the present day. Thus it was that editor Ray Palmer mis-named it "racial memory." So now I shall explain the actual truth of how it came about that the ancient, forgotten past could live today, exactly as it was, in the mind of a modern man myself.

Through scientific, indestructible mechanisms the Ancient Ones' thoughts were recorded on a kind of microfilm, sealed in non-corrosive containers. Placed in one of their thought-record projectors, these records yield more precise and accurate information about that ancient life than any of our history books about more recent events. By the nature of synthetic thought-electric flows given off in strength by these particular mechanisms, the person "reading" the record feels he is himself the person experiencing the occurrences described in the thought-record. The flow of image-bearing energy from the record is so much stronger than one's own energy of consciousness that the experiences produced from the record remain in the mind more vividly than any actual experiences. Thus these records control the mental processes in such a way that the past is lived again in a more vivid fashion than one's own life. These records left by the Elder Folk are a more faithful transcription of actual history than any other records kept since.—Richard Shaver.

being two people at once worry you; it does not last long. This is the greatest experience the ancient wisdom of the caverns can offer you, to read the mighty thought—to actually become as a God of the ancient times."

I saw her throw a Titan-size switch on the wall and in a flash—

* * * *

I WAS not Dick Shaver, but another man entirely. I stood in a forest of tremendous fern trees. Beside me was a long, enormous cylinder of smoking metal, still hot from its recent passage through the upper air. From it emerged a woman, larger than I, and in her arms she carried my child.

The fern trees seemed topless, stretching up until distance made the tremendous fronds seem fragile and delicate to the eye, at last disappearing in the mists. In the sky I could see many similar cylinders and knew they were decelerating and would come to rest at last near us. I knew that we were members of an Atlan* colonizing expedition, sent to this blazing new sun and its planets where life was furiously fecund, capable of developing a crescendo of growth into complex forms that would from our landing onward be guided by our skill and wisdom. My ship was the first to land of the colonizers of planet three under this new star named Sol.

Put the child back in the ship, Lia," I called to the woman. "Then help me get out the materials for our house. The sooner we are safe within its walls the better, for we can't tell what forms of inimical life may have been developed since the tests were made so long ago by the explorers."

"Yes, Lord of my Heart," answered the obedient Lia.

----

*Atlan—one of the three major races of space, the other two being the Titans and the Nortons.—Ed.

The two of us began to haul out from the cargo compartment of our spaceship the sections that enabled us easily to put up the walls of our new home. The walls contained giant spider-web coils, which would set up an impeding magnetic field that would allow only beneficial energy to enter my home. The house walls, once the power was turned into them, set up a huge force field, which allowed only waves of a certain frequency to enter the interior. This particular frequency had been determined upon by exhaustive tests of the beneficial and detrimental content of the electric and magnetic waves sent out by the star, Sol, overhead.

From time to time as I, Duli, and my wife labored over the rapidly rising structure, other spaceships from out of the void drifted down into the great clearing where we had landed first of all upon this planet which we called Lemuria, or, as the surface men refer to her, Earth. These spaceships were full of fellow colonizers, who immediately set about erecting their homes, just as Lila and I were doing. Although many days passed, it seemed that no time at all had passed before the pioneers had settled down into more or less regular living in their new environment.

The days passed most eventfully, for each one brought immense new vistas of the possibilities that lay in the immensely more fecund and different growth from anything we had known.

Within the chambers of that house I knew those beneficial vibrants from that new sun would very soon build up a charge of increasing potency, for the waves could enter, but, due to the direction of the flux of the field in the walls, could not get out again. Thus, the house Lia and I had skillfully constructed became a great trap for beneficial energy and within it we Atlan children would grow very swiftly to great size and immense strength and the best of all, unbounded intelligence.*

I LIVED through what seemed years of time. I saw the cities grow. Over our homes, after a time, we erected domes of crystalline plastic. The air within each dome was not dusty or poisonous, but was a prepared mixture of gases, germless, fortified with health giving nutrients, odorless, super-penetrating, an ever-present agent for physical well being.

The light, always on where needed, never oppressive, was a soft luminosity that possessed a beneficial force all its own, even contributing an additional push to the forces that make life grow in beauty and strength. The natural electric magnetism of earth's force field, which is in itself an agent of integration or growth, was strengthened and focused on the sidewalks and in the living chambers of those wondrous cities

---

*This thought record story, given to Mr. Shaver by Nydia, was a logical one to begin his education into the past history of the Earth, for it depicts the arrival of the first Atlan colonists on the Earth, named by them Lemuria. The reason for colonization was that our sun was then a new sun, still sending out radiations from a carbon fire only, and not from the poisonous metals, radium, uranium, polonium, etc. (the heavy metals), and was thus a healthful place to live. Even so, the colonists built their homes in a manner to keep out the poisons that cause old age, which might be present in some small quantity.

Our sun, today, from which the Atlans fled 12,000 years ago (see "I Remember Lemuria!" in the March, 1945, AMAZING STORIES) because it was causing the disease of old age by projecting minute disintegrances down on the Earth in a steady rain, is the answer to the riddle of death our scientists seek to solve. In water, the poisons are present in heavy suspension, especially in thermal springs; in the air the poison floats forever with the tiny thistledowns of dust it has infected and to which it clings; it settles in the leaves of plants—so that we take the poison in with every drink of water, with every breath, with every bite of food; and as a consequence grow "old" by tissue and cell inability to restore itself fully because of the hindering and ever-present fire of disintegrance from the accumulations of radioactives. Age is nothing but a radium "burn"; a damage to the living cell so that its functions are gradually stopped and retrograded until restoration by normal process is impossible. When the cells can no longer renew themselves, we die.—Ed.

so that the natural rate of integration growth of matter was increased by hidden mechanisms focusing overhead magnetic field lenses.

These field focii were formed where the light and happy feet of our people were led most often in pursuit of that pleasure that we called work.

For work was pleasure to us, in the increasing flood of strength and awareness that in ever greater tide flowed through our limbs. For in these cities of new life age was conquered and youth growth never ceased. When a physical body grew too large to continue living in comfort on earth, these larger beings graduated by stepping into a car, kept at the bottom of a long rock tube pointing at the stars far above. With similar companions they took their places in that space car. Then through them and through the metal body of the car rushed a flow of force, which, countering the friction of the penetrative particles that cause gravity* rendered the car weightless. A small explosion mechanism like a large cap pistol of the repeating type began a gentle hammering on the rear of the car, and weightless as it was the car swiftly gathered momentum, vanishing into space in a moment, for where weight is not present inertia is not present either. So on the reverse flow gravity beam the graduates of Earth rose into space and voyaged through the empty void like a flash of light, presently to slow and circle slowly about another planet, double the size and weight of Earth until the great beams of

----

*The Lemurians say gravity is the result of the condensing (or fall) of infinitely tiny particles of disintegrated matter that fill all space (our scientists call it the ether) into existing matter, such as the Earth is. The friction of these falling particles, falling through matter, causes that "push" we call gravity. These particles Mr. Shaver calls "ex-disintegrance" (or "exd"). Here we see the utilization of some sort of force which neutralizes the friction of gravity, and thus produces weightlessness, with the result that a space ship can be driven against gravity at great speed with only very tiny rocket blasts, like little popguns.—Ed.

reverse flow soon reached up and eased the car down into the heart of another great city, deeper and bigger than the one those beings had left, and much finer, for the builders' minds had broadened as their bodies grew through the centuries.

DULI the pioneer lived a long and active life on the planet Earth and I, Richard, lived it over in my own brain through Duli's recorded thoughts. Duli became an Elder of the ruling council in the city of Barto on the planet Mu*, for he was kindly and wise. Many fine sons did Lia give him and life was one swift stream of pleasure and beauty and hard work that of itself seemed only sport to the ever-increasing strength and intelligence of a being who lived under the amazingly beneficial conditions of Barto on Mu. In Barto the life that was being built up for the people being

But with the passing of years and the increasing growth and size that came with them, arrived also the day when Duli realized that the time had come for him to graduate into a broader life than Mu could offer. He knew that he must leave his sons and the work he had been doing on Mu for a greater planet and its fuller opportunities for life. He stepped into the great spaceliner with Lia at his side...

Blackness then hurled itself down upon those thoughts that had usurped the mind of Richard Shaver. He ceased to exist as an Elder of the Council of Barto on Mu, and returned to the existence of the convict who had escaped from state prison because a blind girl from the caverns had loved him.

* * * *

I, RICHARD SHAVER opened my eyes and felt quite cheerful again under the spell of the little blind witch-maid who was laughing merrily at my bemused awakening.

----

*Mu—an abbreviation for Lemuria.—Ed.

"It puzzles you, Richard, does it not? You have lived over a century of olden days yet here you were, all the time under my eyes. You were but reading in the manner in which we read down here, the record stored in the caves long ago of the life of an ancient Atlantean."

"But it was real. I actually did live it," I protested, almost incredulously. "I must have been that man, Nydia. How else could I have known the most intimate thoughts of his mind?"

She shook her head from side to side, smiling.

"It was real, but not for you, save as you experienced that ancient Atlan's own thoughts. These shelves that line our library here are packed full of such records."

"Have you read them all?" I wondered.

"Yes, Richard all. For I am not contented with a bare existence as it is lived here in the caverns. I long for a fuller, wider life such as those ancients lived. So I have read and studied all these records and they are now part of my own knowledge."

"I was enthusiastic as I glimpsed the possibilities her words opened before me. In that little blonde head was packed knowledge of Earth-life that scientists would give their lives to acquire and place before the surface world. And I, also, could gain that knowledge for myself and perhaps manage somehow, someway to pass it on. Oh, it was a brave thought.

"It is not harmful, then, this reading of old records? No risk is entailed by this vicarious living in strange and perilous scenes?"

"How could there be?" she responded simply. "You sit here, quite relaxed and comfortable, and in your brain alone you live many other lives, acquiring thus those experiences and that knowledge which would otherwise take many, many years of life in many forms to gain. Are you willing to learn more, my Richard? Do you wonder that I care not to spend my life in dalliance with love, heavenly as it is thus to pass the days with you?"

"You are right, my Nydia," I cried, enthused. "How wise you are, dear love!"

The blind girl's strangely thrilling voice continued as I stared at her, my own face all wonder at the seeming magic at her finger's end, that could touch a switch and relieve an existence.

"THIS is stupendous," I stammered, dazed at the vistas of wonder her words opened before me.

"Ponder, my Richard, upon the science you have absorbed from the reading of that one ancient wise man's thoughts as they coursed through your brain. After you have read and thus lived many lives through the records in these caves you will find that there is not a machine down here that you cannot understand and operate. You will even learn something of how they were constructed. Then indeed you will be a most useful member of our little group, for you may then be able to help us devise more efficient ways of outwitting and out-fighting those devilish *dero* I have shown you."

"If you can teach me through these records how to fight those Things you tell me are your bitter enemies, get on with it!" My voice, the voice of Richard Shaver sounded strange in my ears, as though an older, wiser voice had come from my lips.

I felt that to my surface years I had added those other untold years of an ancient Being's wisdom.

"Very well, my Richard. You shall voyage forth again."

Nydia selected a bulky roll of record from the racks and held it so that I could see the words graven on the case. She read them: *Life and Wars of Bar Mehat of Thor, Hero of Three Worlds.*

"You shall live a great hero's life and you shall see and speak with Jormungandur,* the Worm that encircled the world. This is a record of which I am most fond and I have read it often," the blind girl told me.

She slipped the roll into the mechanism and adjusted my headband carefully. Her lips touched mine almost with reverence, so grave was that caress. I sensed that the life of Bar Mehat, the hero, meant much to my little blind maiden.

It was with repressed impatience that I awaited the touch of her finger on the control that was to open for me the door to a more vivid and exciting world.

* * * *

I BECAME another man, a greater being physically. My body was huge yet I was aware that I was very young in actual years. My sturdy legs were cased in knee boots of glistening gold-colored synthetic leather, my body in a skintight covering of overlapping golden scales that formed a flexible protection like armor. Upon my head I wore a scarlet helmet that contained thought detection apparatus, for I heard voices and movements nearby although the chamber where I stood seemed empty. One voice sounded, though afar, particularly peremptory. It was a feminine voice and one that I, Bar Mehat, recognized with a little grimace of half annoyance.

I tossed my head petulantly so that the red-gold hair that fell to my shoulders in shining waves swung loosely with the action. One of my broad, red-haired hands touched the lever of the console before which I stood. A clicking mechanism stopped and was then followed by a steady musical hum like the spinning of a giant top. Dim luminosity pulsed about me. In a four-foot circular mirror above the console a silvery aura

---

*Jormungandur—In Norse legend, a son of Loki. Also known as the Midgard Serpent.—Ed.

flickered madly, to coalesce slowly into the likeness of a young and attractive woman.

Her lips moved and it was then as though she was present in the room with me, for her voice sounded with clarity in my ears.

"Bar, the thing is growing faster than our control of it. It actually threatens all life on our planet. Jormungandur is not a joke."

"Certainly he is no joke; but why fret yourself, who are on land, about Jormungandur who lives in the sea?"

My laugh was loud and free. Women! How they worry over nothing! "As long as he kept to the sea why should I worry about him?" cried the young woman resentfully. "It is because he is creeping up out of the sea that I am disturbed. His body now completely circles the earth. His tentacles have spread over half the unsettled portion of Afrik. They are a hundred leagues long and they grope continually for food."

"That is not so good, fair cousin. His tentacles are entirely too many," I growled.

"He has them along his whole body," cried she. "If he takes a notion to crawl out of the water for a breath of air it means the ruin of all the Atlans' work on Mu."

"Has no one done anything to check the Worm?" asked I, in some wonderment for although the Covenant forbade direct attacks that might result in death, yet there was some allowance for self-defense in cases of unbridled encroachment even against an honored and intelligent ancient like Jormungandur, who was friendly to the early Atlans.

"We have a dozen great dis-rays raving at the tentacles but as fast as we disintegrate them he throws out others. It seems futile even to continue for we get nowhere with all our efforts."

"Jormungandur," I mused aloud. "The Worm that encircles the world. Why, Gracia, he was here before the

Atlans colonized Mu. Mu is practically his property. Are you sure that it is quite legal under the Covenant to attack him, even if the attack seems futile?"

"This is no time for joking, Bar Mehat of Thor," somewhat acidly expostulated the young woman. "Either you agree to bring sufficient military forces to take a planet from Mephisto himself, or you do nothing, and I look elsewhere for assistance against this peril. All my Afrik possessions are now completely under The Worm's tentacles, you—you boudoir decoration!" cried my cousin with scathing implication.

I laughed again. I couldn't help it. Gracia's wrath was so easily aroused, and Gracia at white heat was not hard to look upon.

"I shall arrive to banish The Worm before another sunrise," I promised.

"I trust you are not too sanguine," she snapped. "It will take some doing to banish him, Bar. Farewell until the morrow."

MY HAND reversed the lever. The image of the pretty young woman faded from the surface of the mirror and once again it reflected only my broad face.

I mused to my reflection: "The Worm, a threat to Gods, one should really have known that it would happen some day. Now I, the simple warrior am called upon by my dear cousin to do my duty by my family. And in what a cause!"

My face in the mirror grinned at me wryly.

I thought, that as chief heir of all the possessions of the Province of Thor, I could muster enough military strength to take a planet or even to blast Jormungandur. I addressed myself to the task by pressing a stud marked "General Alarm to Thor Guard" and spoke rapidly and authoritatively.

"Officers of the Thor Guard are to muster all strength at once for an expedition against the Worm Jormungandur who has become a threat by tossing his tentacles over much land in search of food. Anything that can fly or float on water, throw a ray or carry a bomb is to be made ready for extended travel immediately. All available weapons are to be loaded and ready before midnight tonight. Destination Afrik. Bar Mehat speaking."

Through my mind in an undertone to the business now in hand ran the history of the Atlan struggle with growth on this planet of Mu. Under the beneficent rays of the new-born sun nothing aged or ceased growth, and existence had depended therefore, those first centuries of our colonization, upon keeping encyclopedic notes on every form of life on the globe, in order the better to forecast the future development of each species. For as the humble caterpillar changes to the miraculously different moth, so did these new creatures of Mu develop startling metamorphoses and variations. Since none of them died, and since but little of the planet was as yet explored or settled, strange and numerous were the threats to our continued existence which came out of the dense jungles or out of the fathomless depths of the seas, ravening down upon our attempts at an ordered and cultured life.

Most of these tremendous monsters of growth had been slain like the Giant Man, a freakish growth of the earliest days, who had literally attempted to eat everything living on Earth, but had at last been slain by our hero Byrr, and whose body in rotting after death had fouled the atmosphere of the whole planet. Or like Fenris the Wolf, who, before he died had sired a race of giant wolves, which still infested many of the northern forests. The number of giant life forms that made us Atlans trouble were legion, but somehow Jormungandur the Sea Worm had escaped our general war against them. The Worm had always seemed safely confined to the seas and he had moreover agreed to the terms of the Covenant, hence the Worm had never actually been considered as any kind of real threat to existence on Mu, despite the fact that under the fecund rays of the newborn sun his growth would have been predicated as in itself a threat.

THE jungles in which lived those giant variants of life were, if considered for themselves alone, terrifically beautiful dreams of life growth. The trees seemed to grow upward forever, and to be essentially topless. And there was no average size from the tiniest stalk to the trunks of some ancient trees that were acres in extent. They were the result of century after century of completely unimpeded, unchecked growth under completely favorable conditions for life generation. For as yet, nothing had ever really aged and died on Mu.* As most of the spores of life on Mu had originated on distant planets under aging suns rather than by spontaneous generation under the new sun's beneficent

---

*The natural nature of life is to go on living forever. Death is not a part of the scheme of life. It is only the result of radioactive poisoning from an "old" or metallically disintegrating sun. Thus, here on Mu at the time of Bar Mehat, the sun was sending down only beneficial radiations of carbon, which is not a poisonous element, but on the contrary, the basic element of living forms. Thus, nothing grew old, or died, except by actual destruction through accident or through killing. All things, including vegetation, continued to grow so long as there was a source of "raw material" and energy. A living thing grew through two processes: the replenishing of its body cells by transmuting foodstuffs into living cell matter; and by assimilating the disintegrated matter which fills all space and which science today calls the "ether." The reader will remember that it is this, condensing and falling toward all matter (which also includes living beings, naturally) that serves to build up the universe, and as a by-product of its function, causes the phenomenon we know of as gravity, by the friction of its progress through matter.—Ed.

warmth and aura, there were of fruit and flowering a-plenty.*

Those flowers were often of such monstrous size that could stretch myself out in one as in a swaying hammock.

So also all trees tried their best to emulate Ygdrasil.* There were many serpents in the dense forests and in adventuring therein one was likely to run into the giant body of a rainbow-hued reptile of girth too great to climb over and whose head and tail were out of sight in the distance.

The hunger of these things was beyond description, but the supply of every form of life was of an abundance that cannot be even imagined. The monster Scylla by the whirlpool Charybdis; the Worm; the frost giants whom I, Bar Mehat, and my intimates often visited, as had my ancestor, Thor.*

I had recollections of my home city, Atlansgaard, colloquially called Asgard, not far south of Ginnunga Gap, a canyon of abysmal depth to the north and east, separating the civilized area of the Northlands from the Dark Lands, as the wild and practically unexplored land of the Giants was called.

----

*How big the flowers of the under-forest were it is hard for Shaver to judge since surface folk of today measure everything by comparison to the average size of a man, and the Atlans of the new planet Mu had no such criterion. Bar Mehat's size was governed, as was that of other Atlans, by the age of his parents and his own age, two variant factors that resulted in a wide variation in size, which did not run uniform to the years of age, as in modern man.

As nearly as Mr. Shaver can judge, Bar Mehat was about twelve feet high and a very young man at that, as his parents were huge giants of the far planet of Atlan. His years on Mu were under twenty.—Ed.

----

*Ygdrasil—Norse myth: the world tree whose roots and branches bind together heaven, the Earth, and Hell. Today the California redwoods still live, to prove that such monstrous growths once existed.—Ed.

----

*Cerberus, who guarded Hades in the latter days, after the flood had receded and death by old age came upon the world, is well known. But

THE SHAVER MYSTERY, Book Three

these were the later days, that "twilight of the gods" and of their greatest battle, "Ragnarok," when the poison of our aging sun's induction had maddened those who tried to remain on Mu.

It can only be conjectured for surface men, what life was like when the sun was new. Since nothing aged, the forms of life were of mighty, ever-increasing size. The legend of the Worm that encircles the world and to eat must consume his own tail, was probably as near as one could come to any description of sea-monsters whose farther ends would be out of sight when one glimpsed their gaping maws. Men, too, were mighty of size, yet there were some very tiny, the products of a science beyond present-day mankind.

The "seeing rays" of those ancient scientists reached everywhere, and from this our religious faiths have derived their teaching that "God is everywhere." Those rulers were probably widely aware of all near and far surroundings on Mu, for their beneficial rays and potions made them so. They molded life forms to their will. They precipitated energy ash (ether) and from it synthesized the elements they needed most. Space travel was so commonplace with them that they thought of it in the same terms in which we of today think of motor cars.

What we can find of their thought is interesting especially in its multiform concept known for short as MAG-ic, the word being derived from IC, later Greek for science, and M-AG, or Man-augmented. This magic reached its height before two things, both long expected, happened. The carbon layer around the sun burned down to the heavy metal underneath. Sunlight became increasingly poisonous, since it contained minute quantities of disintegrant metals; disintegrant flaming lead, radium, titanium, uranium emanations filled the bright sunlight. Old age, long prophesied, appeared.

Then began the periodic migration to a new, carbon-coated sun. Most of those Elder Folk left Mu for planets of kindlier augury. But some of those brilliant beings, loving "Mu" as they called our mother earth, remained, fighting the poisonous effects of sun metal with their extended knowledge. Before its accumulations could bring on advanced age, they would extract it from their bodies magnetically. Thus, keeping their immortal youth, sheltered in their deep caverns from the heavy metallic induction of our sun, those remnants of the race of immortals stayed on, to be the source of our many legends of the gods. —Author.

Those giants were a race from a *der** planet. They had been shipwrecked on Mu and as yet there had been no particular reason to banish them, driving them back to their home planet. They were comparatively ignorant and as far as we Atlans knew, harmless. They were called Frosts; why, I myself, could not have explained. They were of huge stock, running from thirty to fifty feet in height. I knew that under Mu's non-aging sun their growth would in due course be something terrific and I realized that their existence was a problem that would have to be settled in the not too-far future. There were many such problems and the Atlans were not yet well enough entrenched on Mu to have solved them all satisfactorily. There was much tendency in the life forms of Mu that was alien; it had to be weeded out eventually, since only conflict can be expected from life forms not of the same source pattern as our own.

I EMBARKED on the flagship of the fleet that in a matter of hours was flashing over the tremendous sea of earthy waves that was North Afrik.

Our space ships settled behind a convenient range of mountains over which we could see the tentacles of the Worm writhing like titanic serpents against the morning sky. Here and there blazed the fiercely brilliant orange of powerful disintegrating rays and even at that distance the smell of roasting flesh was noticeable; unpleasantly so. We broke out our smaller scout planes for reconnaissance. I went aboard the foremost, for I wished also to visit my incensed cousin and reassure her that all was well since I and my forces had come into the picture.

As our scout planes shot upward, a long vee of odd planes

----

*Der planet—detrimental energy planet. One on which an aging sun pours its rays, and causes, in addition to age, a mental detriment, insanity. Our Earth, today, is a Der planet.—Ed.

boomed up from the south and shot past our formation in a northerly direction. I had thought I was familiar with every type of plane on Mu, from jet to nose-ray, but the design of those planes was entirely strange to me. They disappeared from my sight, but not from my questing mind. Strange planes above Mu were not to be ignored; their presence might be forerunner of grave trouble.

Within minutes, my arms embraced the very attractive knees of my charming cousin Gracia and her tirade of feminine near-invective poured itself upon my defenseless masculine head.

"Wise Bar, of the blood of the great Thor, could not any fool have foreseen this? Jormungandur, nonetheless, came on the Rolls of the Covenant. Explain that, you feckless dreamer!"

"Sweet cousin," I protested meekly, striving to stem the flood of that aroused ire. "I did not create the Covenant."

"A most fortunate fact that you didn't. Do you know what lies under those reaping arms, blind and stupid one? Do you know what that beast of the abyss of ocean has eaten?"

"Gracia—"

"Ten thousand acres of parasites I developed, to destroy alien plant forms. Now, in one week, that infinitude of belly has destroyed ten years of our best labor."

I tried to block that tirade with a recital of the magnitude of the forces I had headed for the retribution that must necessarily be laid upon the Worm for his rebellious action against the Covenant, behavior code of inter-racial law.

"Look, cousin, I have complied with your wishes. Last night my fleet assembled on the waters of Jotun Bay outside my windows in Asgard. It is a heterogeneous collection, I will admit, but look how little time you've given me to get it together. Glossy jet-planes, Gracia, some submersible fliers, and some heavy-bodied passenger planes to carry men. Not to mention three thousand top fighting men."

She shrugged her shapely shoulders and wrinkled her nose distastefully.

"I notice that you have not brought your armored spaceships, hero."

I was quick to pick up that in rebuttal.

"Because, fair cousin, they are too unwieldy for surface work. Yet, I did dispatch several with large cargoes of foodstuffs and ammunition and other supplies for our base on the Gold Coast."

She heaved a deep sigh of unwilling resignation.

"Oh, I presume you have done the best you knew how," she stabbed.

I COULD not refrain from grinning. Gracia was not a good loser and she had lost out with me thus far, for I had not failed to think of everything at my command that might be needed in that mighty fray that was scheduled to take place between us Atlans and the Worm.

I knew that killing a thing with the growth rate and titanic strength of Jormungandur was not going to be a simple matter. His body encircled the whole Earth and was of incalculable mass.* Its nature was much that of the starfish; break it in twain, and both halves grow. We knew that his great age had developed mental reactions of a kind similar to

----

*Obviously here the description is not an accurate one. By Bar Mehat's own admission, earlier in this thought record, all of Mu (Earth) has not been explored. Apparently the known portion of it (except for casual observation from space ships) consisted only of Europe and Africa, and a portion of Asia, probably just east of the Norse countries. Thus, the Worm, Jormungandur, occupied the Atlantic Ocean between what is now the above-mentioned continents and the continent of Atlantis (also included in the known portions). Its size must have been tremendous, perhaps as much as five hundred miles long.—Ed.

THE SHAVER MYSTERY, Book Three

human thought from the fact that this had been true of other monsters of growth on Mu. I was shortly to learn just how far this mental development of the oldest and most monstrous creature on Mu had been carried by the beneficial rays of the newborn sun.

I returned to my scout plane and thence to the flagship of our air fleet.

My ship was equipped with the mechanisms that would put all space at my command, to be seen and heard and to throw my voice into the ears of those whom I willed to hear it. I had the ship hover over that part of the ocean between the continents of Atlantis and South Afrik, that particular spot where it had been said that men had talked with the Worm many a long day ago. I switched on the vis-ray, and it sank miles deep into the murky depths. At last, after I had turned it hither and yon, there glowed on the visi-screen like twin moons the awful eyes of the most ancient life on Mu.

The telaug revealed his thoughts to me and I pitied him as that river of desperate and weary meaning flowed from the thought cloud like the drifting soul of a lost sea. The Worm was hungry. He was weary of the emptiness of a life that contained nothing but slumber and feeding. His groping tentacles were no longer able to find sufficient food and he was bitterly resentful at a fate, which had given him life, which he found it difficult to sustain, and later had given him thoughts so that he understood what he was. For long I pondered that wretched but intriguing life that was the brain center of the Worm that encircled the earth. At last I spoke, sending my voice to the distant Worm's lair.

"Garm," said I—in Afrik and near parts Jormungandur was called Garm—"Garm, speak to me. Give me an answer, for I am your friend if you will have me so. From the darkness that shrouds you, from the gloom in which you

59

must wallow in the abyss of ocean's depths, speak to me, who wishes you well. It is Bar Mehat of Thor who calls you."

THAT deep river of gloomy meditation ceased its slow flow and concentrating itself reluctantly, looked out of the pale lucent orbs that were Garm's eyes. Great abstract thoughts welled up the ray and flung themselves on the thought-cloud like corpses pushing upward for release from the sucking ooze that clung to them. That husky, thick voice enunciated words with heavy difficulty.

"It is long since Man has sought me out. What would you of Garm?"

"In the old days, Garm, you were one of the few of the serpent race who upheld the Covenant's code. Why have you forsaken the ways of peace? Why are you now unfriendly to Man? Your body is now partly on land, and it is land upon which my family has expended much labor. Now all that constructive work is spoiled and many good men whom in the old days you would have called friends, rejoicing that they lived on Mu, those men have died under your long arms' fatal suctions. Must we then slay you, Garm, that we may live?"

Garm's thoughts moiled over this problem. They flickered back and forth without much consistent form on the thought cloud.

"Once I loved men," he slowly answered at last, his thick voice dull with a kind of indifference that troubled me, the listener. "I loved them for the bright pictures they sent me and for the beautiful children they bore. I loved them for the tales they told me of their lively doings in the sun. But now they have long forgotten me, and I raven for food.

"I am grown too big to feed myself well, even though I draw from the vast seas in which I lie. It may be that you must kill me, for I know not and care not longer what I do.

Life holds no significance for me. I have outgrown life, perhaps."

"Garm, I think that if you will but be reasonable, we may find some way to feed you, so that you may continue to live on," I offered, my emotion being one of real sympathy for a creature so outgrown that we could not by any means within our power send it to a larger planet. Or so I thought at that impulsive moment.

The voice of Garm droned on: "Once a man of your line went a-fishing. Yes, I recognize you for one of Thor's line. For a joke I took the bait between my jaws and raised up my head near his skiff. He was, like all of your blood, a stubborn fellow and he pulled the bottom out of his boat, trying vainly to land me. At least, that was his pretense.

"After I had carried him ashore on my back we talked for a long, lovely time, he sitting on the sand and I with my head lying on the sandy beach beside him. He told me a tale of another such serpent as myself, grown too long for comfortable living on his birthplace, and he predicted that the same fate lay in store for me, unless I found death by some other means. That great serpent encircled earth as do I, and when the time came that abundant food was no longer available, he took his own tail between his jaws and swallowed it, and after many years he died thus.

"It may be that I shall do that thing, though of late I do not love men or their doings."

I PONDERED the great Being's bitter words and at last I spoke thoughtfully.

"You must know something of our thought magic, Garm? If you will do that thing the other great serpent did, we will arrange that before you do it you shall have many weeks of continual pleasure dreams. You shall sense in dreams glorious matings and victorious struggles. We will give you the equivalent of many lives of pleasure.

"This will take much energy that we could well spend elsewhere, but it will be worth that to us to rid us of your overgrowing, enormous appetite that is becoming so destructive. We will pay you in full and you know that we are honorable. You can weigh this thing well. Will you take our word and after your dreams die honorably, a true son of the Covenant?"

"Bar Mehat of Thor," answered the great serpent, "if your dream-makers deal honorably with me, so will I deal with you. And this you cannot have known, that besides yielding up my life there is a thing or two, which I have learned that I will grant you freely without concealment. I know your magic, but your dream makers may weigh the value of their own lives in the balance of their calculation as to what dreams they give me, for I have means of saving them or letting them drift on to death that will seize upon them unawares. Tell them that, O Son of the Past Great, and bid them measure me out abundance of glorious dreams in gratitude."

Thus it was that I talked with the Worm that encircled the world. And thus it came to pass that Garm told me of things that I knew were true, for I had seen that flight of strange planes that headed for the dense forests that we Atlans had thus far left practically unexplored.

"Strange outlanders came over my seas in great ships and hovered long, sending me their promises of many dreams, as you have done. But they did not ask my death, Bar Mehat; they asked my living aid.

"I learned somewhat of their dreams, and their dreams are not my kind of dreams, Bar of the old line of Thor. There is no light laughter, and there are no gallant young ones with them. Their lives have been miseries of everlasting warring. I want no part of such wretched dreams.

"But they had a ray which they can put upon any part of my body and through that ray control me. So when I gave no consent to their supplications, they forced a part of me to lay waste such portions of Afrik as lies between the two great rivers. So, if you seek them out, where they have hidden themselves within the Dark Lands, you will know whence any coming trouble sources."

"I have seen their space ships, Garm. I knew them for outlanders," I exclaimed. "We shall take steps at once."

"THEY mean to take over the Earth and to develop fecundly. They come from a quarantined planet and have somehow eluded the Atlan *der* patrols. They believe they can win over the Mu folk before help can be called in from greater space against them. How they expect to hold Mu against the entire Atlan space navy, once they have won Mu, I fail to understand. But they are stupid, despite their mechanisms of power, and perhaps they think not of it, or expect by crafty trickery to cheat the Atlans into letting them alone on Mu."

An idea flashed into my mind as I stood staring at Garm's vast head, looking into his fierce elder-wise eyes, twin greenish silver moons flickering through sea water.

"Garm, in the caverns where we breed life forms, our technicians have a way of removing the brain from an animal, a living brain, and putting it into a metal bottle where it lives on, fed by fluid foods and synthetic blood. Since you are grown too big for this earth, will you consent that we may put your brain into a bottle and keep it for a record of the past?

"You have certain wisdoms which you can teach youth, and you like the young, laughter-filled folk of our Mu people. Later, after you have grown accustomed to our ways on land, you will have many friends, and later yet some colonizing expedition can take you with them and plant your living brain into a young reptile on some other planet.

"You may live your life over again and again. Do the Der men offer you anything of like value? And in return for this prolongation of your life, will you then aid us against them?"

The limpid mooneyes flickered into near opacity as The Worm concentrated upon this new and far more interesting proposition I had proffered. I waited patiently for his response and felt certain it would be affirmative. After all—

The thick voice came slowly after a long wait. The mooneyes had cleared and shone greenly through the seawater.

"I accept your offer," said the Worm. "I would fain live on and see your brave new worlds that else I might never visit. I am ready to accompany you when you give me the word that you are ready to attack those interlopers from a quarantined planet. I dislike their warring and resent bitterly that the people of Mu must be forced into battles because of them. Yes, Bar Mehat of Thor, I am your ally against them.

"And when the battling is done with, and you have driven them from Mu, then you shall send me first the dreams for which I yearn in my now empty existence. After I have had my fill of dreams, I shall let your technicians take my brain and preserve it as you have said. Some day I shall again live in liberty in the body of another serpent on some greater planet. Yes, Bar Mehat, I agree."

I was overjoyed at Garm's decision for something told me that he would be an ally not to be scorned in the battle that must ensue shortly between my forces and those invaders from a *der* planet.

"I shall call you, then, Garm, when we make our advance," I told him. "You shall follow my forces—"

Something lively sparkled in the great green moons that were the eyes of the Worm.

"I am to wipe up the debris of your victory?" husked Garm, with a note of derision that piqued me a little.

"No, no," I protested half-heartedly.

But Garm's thick throat uttered a kind of snorting laugh.

"Rely upon it, I shall be with you when and wherever you lead," said he enigmatically, and with that our conference ended.

THUS it was that when my forces made ready to advance into the Dark Lands where the invaders had entrenched themselves in expectation of our coming, Garm's tremendous body flowed after the army of Thor's men. The sight of him was comforting as we pressed on into the night of the jungle. Like a mighty river of greenish black flesh encrusted with barnacles and sea plants, the titanic Jormungandur was a reservoir of strength incalculable, in truth of a value of many armies because of those splaying tentacles that absorbed all life they seized upon.

Like the mighty leaders of prior times I strapped to my back my anti-grav packs and flitted ahead with my scouts. These anti-grav packs enabled us to rise to a considerable height above the ground, which was a great advantage in entering that jungle where otherwise we must have been obliged to spend much precious time slashing down the heavy undergrowth. A number of the scouts were to go on ahead, it was arranged, and I flitted not far behind, with another squad of scouts directly in my rear. After these came the main body of our troops. It was while I went on in this way that I saw the girl in the trees, and learned what kind of enemy we had to face.

She was wearing an anti-grav pack and she had depended upon it to escape the swaying head of a monster reptile whose coils layover the rude path that ran for some short distance into the forest. She had apparently no weapons of defense or had lost what she had possessed, in her flight from the great snake. Now she was entangled in the thorny, shielding branches of the tree to which she had flown, and the serpent seemingly did not care to thrash about against those prickly thorns with which it was equipped. I alighted on the branch where the girl clung.

"What has happened? Have you no weapons?"

"It came upon me so suddenly," she faltered, "that I dropped my ray-gun. And what use is a knife against that scaly skin?"

I looked at the reptile. It would have to be eliminated, or its presence would block the advance of my men. Moreover, the creature had set its stupid mind upon capturing what probably seemed to it legitimate prey, and it kept its evil eyes hypnotically upon the girl, who trembled with apprehension.

"The thing must be slain," I said boldly, and let myself down lightly upon the sloping back of the monster snake.

I SCRAMBLED up the scaly back to the bumpy ridge of its spine. Then I pulled my disintegrating ray from the holster and blasted a shot through the center of the spine, severing the spinal cord, I raced lightly, depending upon the anti-grav pack to lift me as I leaped, until I had reached the head of the titanic and maddened reptile. At every alternate bound I blasted another path through the spine, leaving behind as I went a paralyzed column of motionless flesh. As I reached the taper of the mighty neck the great head turned, jaws gaping to slay this stinging insect that had wrought such swift destruction, but with swiftly triggered blasts I cut the last nerves at the base of the head. Red threatening maw and evilly gleaming eyes dropped supinely to the earth.

The girl scrambled lightly down from the tree and threw herself at my feet and flung her arms about my knees, embracing them with heart-felt thanksgiving. There seemed to me no time for amenities and I lifted her face and looked piercingly into her wide blue eyes. It seemed to me that I saw mirrored therein a clean and innocent soul and I felt well rewarded for my strenuous and perilous combat with that monster reptile. I surmised that this girl was an outlaw Atlan, else she would scarcely have been at large in the forests. I asked her directly.

"Yes, I am an outlaw."

I did not care to take time to ask her why, but I did feel that she could be trusted.

"We seek those who drive the great beasts to attack the Atlan cities. Do you know where they have hidden themselves, maiden?"

The girl remained on her knees, but her limpid eyes were raised to mine.

"Are you the leader who seeks those evil people of the dark forest?" she asked.

I nodded in affirmation.

"Had I known that the leader of the forces was so princely, I would never have fled the Atlan cities," said she cryptically.

"This is no time to exchange pleasantries, maiden. Do you know the hidden entrenchments of my enemy?"

"You must be Bar Mehat," she said, ignoring my query.

"I am indeed Bar Mehat of Thor," I assented with impatience.

"Then I am for you. I owe you my life. I belong to the forest people, of whom you must know. We are outlaws and hide always from such as you. Among us came, not too many years ago great ships with many guns."

"I know. But recently I saw some of their space ships and knew invaders had landed on Mu. Go on, maiden."

"They are not like us," said she. "They have skins colored and blotched like lizards. Like the chameleon lizards.

Somewhat on the order of man are they, with four limbs. Their webbed feet have prehensile toes and their hands are long-fingered. They have a long, fleshy tail that tapers to a whip-like point, hanging from their rumps. They have large, flat heads and their eyes are lidless and reptilian, and are covered with a translucent membrane for protection. Oh, how evilly red those eyes can glitter!"

"Their features, maiden. Do they resemble men?"

"Oh, no, Bar Mehat. Their noses are small and flat and their mouths are wide. They have no chins and their teeth are heavy fangs. Oh, they are most horrible to look upon."

I LIFTED her to her feet. "I take it, maiden, that you must be aware from your familiarity with the forest of where these lizard men have entrenched themselves. Is your anti-grav pack in good order? It is? Then come with me," I ordered, and rose in the air to flit ahead of the second squad of scouts that, seeing me in conversation with the girl, had halted in my rear.

So we went on together and as we went the girl continued to tell me of those pirates of space who had escaped from their quarantined planet.

"They promised us forest folk riches and power and security. Many fair promises they made if we would help them drive out you Atlans. They come from the forbidden spaces where death reigns," she shuddered. "They do not worship the dark gods of space as you Atlans and we forest folk do, for they believe in no good thing. They have learned that death has not yet come to Mu and they think that now, before the Atlans are too well settled, they can drive you out and learn to live as the gods live, by studying your cities and the minds of their captives.

"They are very evil and some things they do made me so fearful that I fled into the deeper forest that I might see them no more. Ah, I cannot sleep yet for thinking of their horrible life, their disgusting mottled bodies, the stink of them. And on those who will not go their way they inflict torments, for they hate the way of the Covenant. They are fools and stupid, though, to believe that they could ever win over the wise Atlans who make friends so easily."

We flitted on for a few moments in silence and I pondered much over what the girl had told me.

"You see, Bar Mehat, whenever an Atlan sees how they work, he becomes their enemy automatically, for it is impossible to know when one pleasures or displeases them, so that it is inevitable that one will in the end be tortured to death. Oh, I am glad to see the men of Atlan coming here in force to banish those foul invaders!"

A cry arose from the scouts in the van and we hastened to join them. The cause of the outcry was simple, after all. They had spotted a *dero* hidden like a chameleon against a dark tree trunk, the faint patterning of his lizard-like skin betraying him, for in his perturbation at our approach it turned from rose to purple, to inky black, then again to faint rose. Our men had overpowered him although he was armed with a projectile weapon. The girl touched my arm.

"Did I speak truth, Bar Mehat?" she demanded. "Is he not as I described him?"

He was indeed as she had told me. I examined his weapon with interest. It was a glass-like gun activated by air pressure and fired a tiny, brittle, venom-filled needle that broke on contact, releasing the poison into the veins of the victim. One of the great cats that infrequently lurk nearer the confines of the forest gave me a chance to test the poison. I fired the gun and the cat whirled and then fell as if paralyzed. We saw that it still lived, but was incapable of any action, save that its furious eyes glared upon us whom it had been unable to escape. We later found that the venom was similar in effect to wasp venom in that it permanently paralyzed the victim;* but left him alive for future reference, as it were.

Later, too, we learned that the lizard men had wasp habits in yet other ways, for they, too, kept their victims living for long periods before eating them. I called for an augment helmet and ordered it clapped on the prisoner's flat head. It was a matter of a few minutes only when his thought, with tremendous augmentation, was flowing back over my entire following forces. In this way I knew my men would be aware of just what they were about to engage in deadly conflict.

These lizard creatures had evolved on a small planet under a very large new sun. While it was not a deadly sun, its rays being full of beneficial vibrants, yet its disintegrant induction had been a tremendous factor in their development. Their will to live had been great, but their will to destroy was as full, thus coloring all their thoughts with vicious intent, for the will to destroy and the disintegrant electric forces are one and the same. While the seed of greatness was perhaps within them, it had been buried irretrievably beneath a rigid discipline of the revolting kind which allowed the individual little personal freedom save the inherent right to reproduce.*

---

*The venom of the wasp is shown on stung spiders, when it destroys the nervous system but leaves the spider living, perhaps conscious, to be eaten later alive by the wasp grub, a system of food storage.—Ed.

---

*In Atlan language there are three kinds of men: *tero,* normal man; *dero,* evil man, and *zero,* useless man. These lizard people were for the most part *zero.* Equal parts of good and evil in the character made their total effect in life merely a repetition of the status quo. But they were foolish enough to allow domination by the *dero,* which rendered the total effect detrimental to all other beings and their own true interests as well. Just so has Hitler, a *dero,* caused the weight of an entire nation of men to be thrown on the detrimental side of the scales. Other men are not smart enough, or well enough intentioned, to remove one Hitler. Notice the world conflagration resulting from the devotion of one nation to a detrimental energy robot.—Author.

WE HAD barely finished the broadcast of the lizard man's thoughts when a tremendous crystal sphere sailed overhead and paused above the midst of our array, for by now my forces had caught up with our scouting vanguard. Then, with a loud report, it flew asunder and there rained down upon us tiny slivers of light that seemed faery spears, playing in all directions. At least a dozen of my best men fell sprawling to the ground as if paralyzed and at that we all knew what had been in that crystal sphere. It was a bomb, full of compressed air and packed with tiny glass capsule needles of the paralyzing venom of the lizard men. It was a most effective weapon and we could not, unfortunately, determine its exact source at that moment.

After that first one, sphere after sphere hissed down upon us through the air and Atlan's bravest fell in windrows. Some of our men thought it a good idea to pick off the spheres with disintegrating ray rifles, but this resulted in the bombs bursting high in the sky, only to rain the venomous needles more widely upon our heads. I had ordered huge disintegrators, mounted high on trucks at our rear, to drop sweeping fans of destruction into the forest ahead of us. Their range was almost incredible, so that fires of many miles in width sprang up ahead. At long last the spheres decreased in numbers and I felt that our rays must have destroyed some station from which they had been dispatched.

I had been well aware that to use a large disintegrator in the jungle was an infraction of the Covenant's code, but if any intelligent life existed simultaneously with those lizard men in the jungle ahead, it was self-doomed by failure to warn us Atlans of the impending attack. All rules are tossed overboard in war, sooner or later. That forest fire, which under ordinary circumstances would never have been allowed to rage, among those trees so big that a man could hardly grasp their immensity even with his imagination, was a sight never to be forgotten.

We Atlans have a curious way of putting out such fires. We have an atomized carbon ray, which we spray into the downdrafts around the flames. This is activated carbon, more inflammable than ordinary carbon, and divided with extreme fineness so that its particles are driven along by certain waves of light. Thus an atomic carbon ray is formed which is sprayed over the fire. The carbon did not, as might be thought, increase the intensity of the fire, for the finely divided carbon combines with the oxygen of the air, blanketing the whole area with carbon dioxide, so as the rays swept the fire ahead, it died.*

AS THE fire broke a way through, my forces marched, leaped or soared over the smoking jungle. To the danger from the enemy army that must be ahead was added that of falling limbs from the great trees that stretched a mile overhead. Some of those giants, remnants of the first early growths, were six or seven miles tall. These gargantuan trees now stood blacked at the base, and at infrequent intervals limbs as long as several city blocks and weighing from twenty to a hundred tons would crash near us. Once in a while the smoldering embers would burst into flame that would leap skyward through the now dried-out framework of lower limbs, but a few well-directed sweeps of the atomic carbon rays extinguished these as fast as they sprang up.

It was a relief to all my thirsty, soot-covered men, when we sighted the enemy's camps. Uttering shrill cries calculated to fill us with apprehension, the lizard men at once set up a barrage of venom glass needles to halt our advance. Here I had made some preparations, which I believed might be the

---

*Apparently the heat of the combination was lost by its dispersion.— Ed.

answer to that type of attack. Forewarned by our prior experience I had ordered that some of our huge disintegrators en route, approximately a hundred, be adapted to prepare from their rays what is called a wind-ray. This is a dual ionizing ray, one ray positively ionizing the air and another negatively ionizing the air. When the rays are held far apart a gentle breeze springs up between them as the molecules of air, drawn by the attracting charges they bear, rush down to neutralize their charge and are pushed aside or spread by the outer inrushing air. When they are held closely together and highly energized, a terrible vortex of inrushing and up-rushing wind is formed. These hastily adapted devices were posted like horns of a crescent on either side of our advancing lines.

As the first crystal gloves hissed overhead, these wind-rays swung into action. Thus the globes, instead of falling, shot into the air like rubber balls on a tossing fountain and, juggling them like circus performers, our expert ray men flung them back into the air over the enemy's camp and then released them, to harry our tormentors by their own venomous weapons. This return barrage was greeted by howls of dismay from the lizard men as their own pigeons came home to roost.

Our penetras* came into action also, sweeping over the whole area in our van, so that whatever was opaque became transparent. What had seemed to be merely earth and forest growth for half a mile ahead of my forces was revealed, so that we saw and knew what the lizard men were keeping behind walls. In fact, the penetra rays were so powerful that for miles ahead the whole enemy work lay revealed as if we saw it through glass. This was done by bathing the whole area in penetrative rays of a nondestructive nature and

---

*Penetra—visi-rays which penetrate and make transparent any object on which they are trained. Thus, in projecting visi-rays through earth, the penetra is used as a carrier ray.—Ed.

sweeping over this with other rays that carried finely divided selenium and other chemicals in the same way that our fire-extinguisher rays carry carbon. These luminosity rays act in the same manner that stains act on a transparent organism under the microscope, bringing out the details in different colors.

WHAT we beheld was most intriguing to my forces. The men bellowed with huge guffaws over the outlanders' methods. In improvised underground pens they had collected overgrown monsters of every description. Held in those narrow tunnels, and fed but little for a long period, these creatures had become ravenous with bestial hunger. Various types of disintegrating rays and venom-ball throwers, as well as other weapons the nature of which was strange to us then, had been attached to the animals' backs. The purpose of this arrangement was obscure until the lizard men threw open the barred doors to the tunnels.

Out rushed the herd of maddened beasts. Mammoths, titanotheres, titanosaurs, dinosaurs and huge serpents rushed down upon us. The ray apparatus on their backs was automatic, sending a beam in a wide arc ahead of the beasts. This beam, a dual ionizer like our wind-ray, completed the circuit when it struck metal. It was then that we realized the new peril we were encountering. The resulting flow of current through the beam activated the firing mechanism for the disintegrating ray. Since all our weapons were fabricated of metal, while those of the lizard men were made out of glass or plastic, these enraged living ray-tanks loosed upon us were more than a subject for laughter, as we had thought when we first saw them through the walls of their tunnels.

At first we held off the terrific onslaught. Our superb gunners picked off the beasts as rapidly as they approached within range, yet the heavy discharges released into the air began to blanket the whole fighting area with a stifling, thought-blocking disintegrating charge. One could hardly move one's limbs because of the effect of this detrimental electric, which leaped like Hell-fires from every bush, every piece of metal, every blade of grass making the vision hollow with the disillusion of despair.

It was not long before our fire was slowed by this subtle nerve-paralyzing influence and the beasts pounded nearer in overpowering numbers, their combined weights shaking the earth beneath us, their great maws roaring, and over their fierce heads flashed ever the automatic fire rays, every flash marking a hit on some metal weapon of ours. Whether this was defeat, or whether the disillusion from the strong detrimental that so subtly held our minds under its potent spell was powerful enough to check our aggressive action, things began to look very dark for Mu. And then—

OVER our cowering heads reared the vast bulk of The Worm. No metal to complete a circuit in that engine of destruction! His curling, mile-long tentacles lashed out, and every beast they touched was caught up, crushed, and tossed aside, a menace no longer. He was the most awe-inspiring being I had ever seen, with the great moons of his eyes reflecting his fierce battle joy. One could almost hear the thought in his vast dragonhead:

"After all these dull, uneventful centuries, what bliss to fight again for the sons of the friends of my youth! Yea! It is good!" From the throat of Garm a great rumbling roar issued and seemed to shape into words. "On, Atlans! On, Atlans!" And the mighty serpent hiss terminated the roaring words.

The great Worm's bulk blotted the sun from overhead so that we fought in the shade as though twilight had descended upon us. From our van we could see the planes of the lizard men taking to the air as they retreated in mad rout from this unconquerable serpent of the ancient days long past. For following upon the appearance of Garm the invaders were, for the most part, speeding away, leaving behind them their dead and wounded and the blazing ruins of their camp. The maddened beasts which they had starved and then released upon us were careening off in all directions for the control rays that had kept them advancing upon us in attack now stood abandoned, their tall masts no longer flashing with energy sparks. The battle was over, save that a few of our fastest planes trailed the fugitive enemy, their purpose not to do battle, but to determine the destination of the lizard men that we might report it to the Space Police.

We bivouacked amid jubilant cries of triumph.

IT WAS some days later that our battered columns wound slowly back into the green cultivated areas surrounding my cousin Gracia's white marble mansion. As we marched we could see in the far distance Garm's acres of scaly body flowing swiftly into the sea. I sped on in advance of my forces, by the aid of my anti-grav pack, and came to a stop at the marble steps, where my cousin stood awaiting me and on my ears again fell the unending recriminations of her anger.

"How could you have let those ignorant, undeveloped idiots from a *der* planet so nearly defeat you, Bar Mehat? Jormungandur himself hardly saved you from destruction. How could you have marched into the face of that ominous situation without preparation, without any special weapons, without prior scouting and information—?"

Her voice went on and on, and I began to think that she was probably right and I an impractical dreamer, unfit to head the troops of Atlan. My too-costly victory told this as well as did the faces of those of my most valued men who still lived.

"I know not, cousin. Youth and ignorance of such traps may be my only excuses," I told her stupidly, for my heart was sick, now that all was well over, at thought of those dead we had left behind in the Dark Lands. "I cannot think of anything else," I apologized.

"It might be well if you did a little thinking, nevertheless, Bar. The Space Patrol is on its way. When it arrives one of its officers will take charge here in command of our Atlan forces and you—you are going back on one of their ships, for you have signally failed to distinguish yourself on Mu. When you are back on Atlan, my cousin, you had best go to the College for Warriors and learn a little something of how to take care of yourself and safeguard your men when you lead them."

I stood with head hanging, for I had no words to give her. She was probably in the right, I thought. I would enter the College for Warriors upon my return to Atlan and I would study diligently and prepare myself in the latest military science so that Mu would be better for my leadership when I returned to that planet.

*   *   *   *

AS I stood, suddenly blackness rushed down upon me and I knew no more of my cousin, or of Garm slowly withdrawing into the sea, or of anything until a light flashed through the darkness and I became aware of an odd popping sound as of a suddenly released run-down record.

I wakened to the soft laughter of the blind maiden as she switched off the thought record reading machine.

Her hands fell light on my shoulders and she leaned to kiss my forehead before she removed the apparatus from my head.

"The record film broke," she told me regretfully. "They are so very old, it is surprising they have lasted so long.

Perhaps it is of little consequence, after all, for that record of Bar Mehat ends when he returns to Atlan."

The faint sound of a gong rang through the cave and we took each other's hands and went together to the dining-hall where the entire group customarily met for meals. I was for hours in a kind of daze, for it seemed to me that I was still Bar Mehat and not Richard Shaver.

Later I realized the lessons from that life I had vicariously lived. It was that anger and warfare, struggle and death, are the fatal fruits of *der,* and *der* was the distortion of the magnetic fields of the thought cells of a mind by disintegrant electric. And Mu in those earlier days had not turned inductively under the new sun long enough to induct the great charge of detrimental electric which makes our life today the hell it really is. It is not good to be a man on a quarantined planet of *der.* If one reads the ancient books that exist always in these old, abandoned planets, one learns that life away from an aging sun is immortal life, while on a *der* planet it is a brief moment of existence and thought under a blasting sun of death.

As this knowledge sank into my mind from the great brain back of Bar's thought-record, a terrible despondency seized upon me. I realized that Earth was now such an outworn living place, quarantined from the great immortal life of space because *der* means warring and men of earth think *der* thoughts. If only we could build again such houses as the Atlans built, which barred the entry of all detrimental energy flows, or even live in caves as did the later Atlans to shield themselves from a deadly sun, we might become again something more than the mere insects we now are.

AS MATTERS now stand, I have become one of the underworld, of those who have been called trolls, gnomes and goblins in the old days. We are the same today and still my friends here fear surface men. For man cannot understand or believe any other form of human life but his own, and they fear us greatly when they learn of our existence. Yet those of us who are kindly intentioned need man's understanding and assistance, for our lives are struggles for existence against the malefic schemes and powers of the evil and idiot denizens of the caverns. Because I realize the tremendous importance of our continued existence as an intelligent group, I have thrown in with Nydia's little band. Nightly I stand watch against the devils who have made their homes in the farther caves. Our life has a price of never-failing vigilance. We peer over the old visi-rays, focusing them to the farthest range and sweeping the caves with them for the slightest indication of attack, that we may turn it back before it reaches us. Daily I spend much time reading the thought records, bringing to my knowledge the lives of the mighty, ancient God-race that existed immortally before our sun aged and they ventured elsewhere. The tale of that aging sun and of the flight of the Elders from its effects is written in those many ancient thought records.* For as the sun ages it

----

* It is this record that was presented by Mr. Shaver in his first story, "I Remember Lemuria!" published in the March, 1945 issue of AMAZING STORIES. When Mr. Shaver presented it to us, he did not explain how he knew it, except in the manner described in the opening of this second story, as a mental impulse from underground minds received at first via his welding gun in a Detroit auto plant. Ignorant as your editor was of the real facts surrounding Mr. Shaver's story, we decided to call it "racial memory" to make it more credible to our readers. We are forced now to retract that, and to admit also, that your editor was the most doubting of all Thomases at the beginning. However, when you read the amazing reactions to this first story, published in Discussions, in the new special section devoted to reporting readers' discoveries and reports on Mr. Shaver's Lemurian story, and in the Editor's Observatory, you will be faced with the same amazing facts which have made your editor look. a little silly for having perhaps harmed the credibility of an incredible story by trying to make it less incredible.—Ed.

grows more dense and as it becomes denser it throws deadly fiery particles out with its light beams. These gather in the body and like radium they never cease to burn; they are atomic fire and deadly in their final result. In time their accumulation burns and withers life away, just as radium would do if we swallowed it. Only ignorant men, who could not flee into space, remained here on earth to father modern man, for the Immortals abandoned their out-grown dwelling places here when they took to their space-ships and flew away to settle under more favorable conditions on other planets.

It is my constant hope that some day Earthmen will waken to the existence of these ancient cavern dwellings, full of marvelous machines and secrets of science infinitely greater than theirs.

It is full time that mankind awoke. I live on only in that hope. Until then, I bid the surface Earth farewell. I remain here in the caverns, absorbing wisdom against that day, and loving (as only those can love who live under the rays of the ancient mech) my little blind maiden.

—Richard S. Shaver*

----

*Actually, Mr. Shaver is no longer in the caverns, but back on the surface, as we shall have occasion to demonstrate later on; but Mr. Shaver intends to present in each issue from now on, one of the "thought record" stories that he listened to while in the caves—and thus, for continuity, we have ended this story where it should properly end, in the caves, with more to come.—Ed.

THE END!

The Masked World
—Originally edited by Raymond A. Palmer—

An incredible revelation of the world of horror hidden beneath modern New York; the caverns of the dero.

"SEVENTEEN DIE, ONE HUNDRED INJURED IN PASSENGER WRECK!

Second part of Great Northern Empire Builder plows into first part of train at Michigan, North Dakota..."

That came over my radio at two o'clock on the morning of Aug. 10. I returned to my typewriter resolved that this time I would really lift the veil from the mad cavern world called "The Masked World."

I know what caused the wreck. I know that many a high-placed man in America knows too just what caused that wreck and many another like it—and sheer craven fear keeps them from telling the world. Well, Shaver is not afraid to tell you why the Great Northern Empire Builder plowed into the forward part of the train on the morning of Aug. 10.

Under that part of North Dakota lies a great cavern highway. It is a highway that stretches clear across Pennsylvania to New York City. In the other direction it reaches nearly to the Colorado without a break. Under that wreck—which happened over a temporarily deserted stretch of this highway, the ancient, time-forgotten underworld road—a vehicle that looks somewhat like a modern living trailer is parked under the loom of a great machine. This machine is shaped like a tremendous human figure with six arms. (Machines of the ancients were often built in sculptural forms; why I don't know.)

Beside the mighty, enigmatic work of a machine art long lost on earth, a little cooking fire gleams. Beside the fire squats a small four-limbed monstrosity. If we look closely his resemblance to man becomes apparent. He *is* human, a very degenerate human, son of the degenerate nomads of the caverns. There are many of his kind, but thank God, not too many.

His ancient rolling home is a living-rollat, a vehicle used by the ancients for just that purpose for which he is using it—a rolling home. It is driven by a motor that requires only an occasional quart of water for fuel. Built of the imperishable metal which the ancients used so universally that much of their work still survives in the hot dry air of the caves, the rollats still roll over the hidden highways; though their passengers and drivers are distinctly *not* the God race that built the roads and the vast machine civilization. I will describe the little ghoul and his relation to the wreck of the passenger train will get clearer.

His name is Max, and he has grown up in the wild bands of gypsy-like marauders who make life in the caves so hazardous. Stopping by the statue to cook his meal, he had turned the studs in the bottom of the great machine. A round screen that was part of the base of the statue had glowed into life, and the beam that shot up from its vast forehead penetrated the two miles of rock overhead and revealed the Empire Builder, overhead on its way through the night.

This particular little ghoul had developed an alleviant for his frequent periods of aloneness, an exciting little trick of wrecking trains. He indulged this penchant whenever chance offered. With the many diverse beams of power built into such intricate old machines by the masterminds of the ancients, and learned by the ghoul through the years of contact with the wandering, wild and frequently wholly evil groups in the caverns' vastnesses (and by his continual poking and prying at the levers and buttons activating the old mech) he soon had the signals set far ahead of the flying train. With a black "shorter" ray he silenced the red signals along the track by shorting the wires feeding the current to the bulbs (it is a conductive ray that grounds any electric it touches—like the Grindell-Mathews ray). It was not stopped nor impeded by the miles of solid rock above Max's head, for like radio waves it was wholly penetrative. Other similar rays can be used to send current into a light that is supposed to be shut off. Thus the evil, little ghoul reversed the signals for the train.

The engineer, seeing the all clear signals, plowed at full speed into the forward half of the two-part train, for Max had carefully reversed the lights for this half of the train, and the engineer was chafing at the red lights that seemed to have permanently decided that time did not matter. Max loved this little trick, and had perhaps a half dozen trains to his credit.

There are many others like Max! Seventeen men died to please the mad little nomad of the caverns; and he laughed and laughed, for he considered this proved that he, Max, the despised of the cavern peoples, was wiser and more clever than the great people overhead. He hated them! What pleasure it was to play the telaug beam over the struggling people as the great weights of the heavy passenger coaches rose on end and fell, crushing, pinning and smashing the people to a bloody mess. Yes, he would wreck many more trains before he was through.

And he will! And many men beside myself know of such things, and cannot tell—or will not—for fear of ridicule.

MAX shut off the power in the mech within the great sculpture, wondering idly as he did so why the old ones had built the machines into great statues that looked like giant people with many arms and great luminous eyes. Remembering that the trader in Ontal would give him food supplies to fill the food bins in his rollat home for jewels like these that gleamed in the great idol's head—he crawled painfully up the smooth limbs of the statue and pried out the eyes. That they were gems worth a great deal more than he would get for them from the trade store, he knew—but what could he do about it? The big shots had the trade sewed up tight.

Crawling down, Max washed perfunctorily and unsuccessfully at the little streams of water that still played from a stone girl that was a fountain beside the highway, grinned a rotten-toothed grin at his own cleverness, climbed like an evil crab into the great machine that was his rolling home. He had to use several great cushions to reach the giant's steering wheel, and adjusting these, he set out.

Max was on his way to the feast of the Sabbath in mighty old Ontal—a long, long way from North Dakota. Max belonged to a cult of Satanists that was as old in the caverns as was history on the surface. Every year, in Ontal, the great city under New York, the Cult members would be feted by the leader of the Cult of the Dark One. It was a yearly event which every nomad attended because it was almost the only time they could enter the city with safety—for at that time safe-conduct was guaranteed by the Cult Leader.

There they were feted by the men who profited most from the use of the organization to their evil ends, and there every sadistic instinct of the hereditary character of some groups of the cavern wights was gratified.

Naturally, everyone knew that the custom of bringing gifts of great value for the great god of Evil was the real reason for the survival of the yearly feast, but where evil pleasure is so lavishly dispensed as it was at the feast of the Devils, the toll was no objection. No real devil could resist the annual feast of Satan. The rulers of the palace of the "Stem" had for two centuries, here in the new world (and for no-one knows how many centuries in the Old Country) counted on the feast of Satan to replenish their coffers, and they were never disappointed. What was the painful death of a few slaves and a stolen babe or two beside the pile of golden objects and gem-set articles the anticipation of the Cultists made them bring from the hidden, lost treasure stores in the uncharted caves?

Max's eyes glittered with anticipation as his mind conjured up the scenes of last year's feast; when the blood-dabbled body of the priestess arose from her prostrate position as the altar before the Red Statue and the great metal body of the old God of Evil itself had arisen and pursued her fleeing form amorously about the Hall in the dance of the Love Death; when the girl on the cross began to drip blood down upon the feasters; when the great red metal God took the priestess in his arms before them all; and when the great stim beam spread over the whole hall and they all writhed in insupportable ecstasy, all together, slave girls and wild nomads. Mad women from the Mexican caverns with madder witches from the far north, nomads from the western states, and the fat little hermaphrodite things from the southwest, the dark men of the Wast clan; all the varied and mad life in the caverns that served the devil. All writhed together under the terrible ecstatic strength of the super-stim that is the most powerful nerve ray on earth. "Roll, wheels!" thought Max. "Soon I will again see the scenes that delight the evil heart as do no others."

Driving all night and the next day along the roads through solid rock that are not equaled by all our vaunted modern science or even approached in excellence—Max drew nearer and nearer to subterranean New York.

CHAPTER TWO
The City of Ontal

WITHIN the dense archean basalt that upholds our modern surface U.S.A.—deep within the solidity of dark rock where no water can ever penetrate, lies a city. It is not so well known as modern New York directly overhead, but it has its friends, its enemies, and its slums—its lords and plutocrats. It is a part of the ancient, forgotten underworld, not entirely unknown to surface man, but unrecognized as a terrible truth, a harmful factor, of his life. Ontal is a part of the civilization under our feet that is called "The Masked World" by those who know.

The underworld is an intricate maze of many levels of titanic caverns, which reach everywhere under the surface of our modern surface world. But under New York the ancient highways that are in reality all part of one vast old planet-city that the earth once was before it had a sun—here the ancient highways converge into a greater city of dwellings than anywhere else in the east. Once this city was called "Bakt" by the ancients—but the part that is lived in today is called Ontal after certain great works in it by that ancient name. It is this city which Max approaches in his big old rollat.

Lately this lived-in part of the ancient underworld is called "Bonur's hole." Those who have brains enough to hate the men who rule the great, gloomy tomb in the last ten years have named it thus. For Bonur Golz is the boss of the "ray bunch" who wring the last drop of tribute from all the life of the ancient city, from all the area supplied by the "Stem," an area as big as several states on the surface, though sparsely populated by our standards.

Bonur's stronghold is a tremendous series of borings that surround the master highway of the Eastern caverns. This highway is called the "Stem" because it is one of the very few highways that connect with entrances to the upperworld. The underworld is so vast that little of it contains life, and not much has even been fully explored. However nigh half of the scattered communities for hundreds of miles around Ontal depend in a large part on the trucks that roll down the "Stem" from the great warehouses of surface New York.

That these trucks are unknown to New Yorkers is not surprising, for they do not go out on the surface often, and when they do they are no different in appearance than other trucks. For though some of the ancient cave conveyances called rollats are used by such as Max, modern trucks from U. S. factories are chiefly used. A certain amount of the produce that enters New York finds its way down the "Stem," and who is to say where everything that enters New York may go? Bonur Golz and his gang hold the strings that control this flow of vitally necessary foodstuffs and commodities.

There are other entrances to the vast underworld than this same "Stem," but they are far away, and open upon primitive communities of no resources, unable to supply the needs of the underworld except in slight part. If they were important, Bonur's fighters would soon obliterate the life with the great disrays that are their weapons, and blow up the entrances so that no food came into the eastern underworld that did not pay his tax.

"RED" Nake is the top man of Bonur's bunch. He has held on to a slippery job for ten years. Nake is a sharp man. A strong slim body, on two long, thin legs; a sharp-nosed face always rusted with the stubble of his red beard; a too-wide mouth set with great, yellow dog teeth; and an evil laugh that sounds much too often, too high-pitched to be pleasant, ever.

Just now Nake is preparing a trap for the unwary rich returning to Ontal from the far southern pleasure spot called by words that carry the ancient name-sounds Sable Base, though what "sable base" may have meant phonetically in the old language no one knows today.

Sable Base was an ancient pleasure spot for the race who had built these vast city caverns over all earth's underrock—and then left earth and most of their work behind. Today the ancient, intricate playthings of the God-race still are used by the modern cavern dwellers—for the same purposes for which they were designed. Imagine a Coney-island built by super-minds of a technical advancement a million years beyond our own—and with the wealth of a vast society to lavish on the building. It had been a great nursery for children mayhap—one cannot imagine serious-minded people playing their lives away in such a place. But when one has seen and experienced the thrills of Sable Base one *can* imagine it...

Intricate mirror mazes interspersed with super-stim impulses that lead on and on into the heart of the maze and in the heart of the maze one finds an opening into a great pool for swimming. An artificial Eden where the water itself is charged with synthetic pleasure nerve impulses—and the persons wandering through the maze take to the water and feel nigh to dying of the intense pleasure it gives them.

Whirling rollat cars with synchronized dream projection for those seated to travel through infinitudes of wonder-lands without ever leaving their circle of travel in reality—and everything that any super-mind could wish for happens to those who ride the chariots—as actually as though it were not a dream!

Such devices and pleasure palaces were innumerable and Sable Base was a pleasure spot where all the rich of the whole Masked World went when they could afford the time; and that was often, for did not the slaves keep them well supplied with leisure time. They had their customary periods for visiting Sable Base, and now a great multitude of these pleasure seekers were winding back over the ancient tube roads toward the vast city of Ontal, which was only populated under part of our New York.

RED Nake planned his trap well. Many of these returning people had things of value which his boss, Bonur Golz, coveted.

Female slaves of beauty and price, antique super-stim mech of the superior kind that only those families had acquired who had the knowledge to seek them for generations in the endless corridors of the world that lies in the darkness of the depths. Jewels that could be sold to the surface merchants—and the greater jewels that only the buyers who come infrequently from far space could afford to buy. Stores of gold, stocks in surface corporations—many things they had that Bonur could take to make himself even more powerful than he was.

So, some twenty miles south of where the old highway debouched into the great bowl of rock that was Ontal proper— the heart of the ancient vastness that had been the God-city called Bakt—Nake set his trap, a double-circle of penetray weapons about the road that is called Ontal-way.

The use of these ancient weapons is an intricate art for they have such range, such maneuverability, and form such intricate interlocking patterns of vast range and power. Such instant obedience to even the weak hands of modern man they have that a man like Nake must make many provisions to assure his own safety from those who might wish to kill him from among his forces. He does this by facing them all in the same general direction in a great arc and welding the swinging snouts' range of movement to a small segment of a circle. He gets behind this sickle of weapons, an arc of vast ray power-of-fire some thirty to sixty miles in range—with his own longer range piece of the most powerful master-weapon he has been able to acquire. Behind him is always three or four of his most trusted knaves, and neither can they swing their weapons upon his back—for that is provided for also. Thus surrounded by the great old ray which is as yet an undefeated weapon on Earth—used for unknown eons in such struggles—and himself at the lever of a weapon of vaster power than any other he has ever heard of in all the vast unexplored underworld from all the wandering, snooping nomads (or from any of the techs that search always for the treasure that is the priceless better sorts of antique mechanisms) Nake can feel quite safe. For no ray can approach him from any direction without first passing progressively more and powerful sets of ray beams of both offensive and defensive nature.*****

At last Nake considers that all is ready, and they wait for a good bunch to collect under their ray beams before exposing their presence. One by one the rollats and incongruously different modern trucks and trailers and limousines from the surface trade collect before him, while the occupants are entertained with all manner of outrageous lies as to the reason for the delay.

Nake opened his wide gash of a mouth to say: "A goodly haul we'll make from this batch of overstuffed ninnys, eh?"

"Aye, Nake, and why should they feel so safe? Why should they

----

*There are many types of beams—shorter types for defense that "short" the offensive rays—and destructive rays of the "dis" type of many kinds.

This sort of trap is called a "cruel" in the underworld and it is truly a "cruel" sight to see the unsuspecting underworld people herded together under the ray beams and slaughtered wholesale. It is accompanied by a kind of thought-tamper as peculiar to it as baseball "talk" is to a baseball game. The victims are told strings of lies— they are safe and among friends;" "just wait and all will be well;" or they are "about to be killed" because of some preposterous charge of obscene nature which is outlined mentally to their fear-struck minds—etc. etc.—all very entertaining to the cruel marauders who practice the "cruel", and vastly tormenting to the victims who know they are doomed to torture and slavery at the very least. –Author think their goods and slaves and wealth should *not* be stolen? An' they were not fools they would not be here so woefully under-armed. There is no place for fools on this wild earth."

CHAPTER THREE
Bonur Golz, Fat Ruler

BONUR GOLZ is very big—very fat and strong—with a great red face and a black stubble always bristling slovenly round his sagging jowls. His lips are big and loose and very scarlet. His eyes are nearly hidden in the fat of his face. His clothes would seem curious to you who have not visited Ontal under New York. They are not modern clothes. They are often the clothes our ancestors wore in medieval times when they knew less than we think we know, and much more than we really do know about the ways called witchcraft. Bonur sometimes wore the clothes of the surface peoples, but he preferred the loose and antique-styled eastern robes fastened about the waist with a soft girdle—in which he could thrust a number of the potent but too large antique hand weapons, just in case.

Bonur is big and fat and strong, and tonight he sits as usual dwarfed by the immensity of the ancient Titan's throne he has used as his own since he took over the Palace of the Stem.

Once that throne was the seat of a Titan of the God race that built the underworld. The vast entity who built that throne for his seat had imbued it with his own mighty dignity so that something of that God-like quality hangs still about the carven stone and gilds the ugly body of Bonur with a grotesque gravity, an incongruous aura of omnipotence.

The great embroidered flowers on his silken robe glow lewdly in the soft light of the mighty cavern where the throne is the central note in a terrible symphony of vanished majesty and might carved from the ageless stone walls with their caryatids shaped like the forgotten giants of a more fortunate, vaster human race. This symphony of terrific, enigmatic and wholly alien beauty led in all its lines to the throne and thus to the emphasizing of the ugly sensuousity of Bonur's ugly body, its grossness wrapped in the glowing, florid silk so that he was the horribly ugly central motif of the whole tremendous scene. His hairy legs stick bare and lewd from under his robe, his eyes behind the rolls of piggish fat glitter as he watches the great valves, oversize entrances, built for a mightier and nobler race than the rats that now sheltered there, for those for whom he waits.

Bonur is waiting for Nake and his men to report on the results of the job he had given them. It was not a nice job, but the men he had chosen were used to that. A series of muffled sounds filtered through the air of the caves from some place not far off.

Bonur grinned, baring his yellow teeth, as he counted the sounds. The same number of great old cargo rollats he had sent out had returned. That meant a great deal to Bonur.

INTO the vast, curiously decorated chamber that was as alien to the mind of modern man as was such as Bonur revolting—into this titanic setting for the evil grossness that was Bonur's self—strode three clanking figures. They were clad in the bad-fitting, cut-down suits of ray-proof armor of the ancients. Off from their necks they lifted the too-big helmets, made of forgotten metal. The motion bared their faces.

Three dark, long-nosed visages, almost alike, so that at first glance the men might be mistaken for Red Nake's brothers. They were not brothers; they were of a race called sometimes, in olden times, "trolls" by the Europeans, though they were never confined to Europe even in medieval and ancient times. That old race of warlocks and underworld mysteries has much the same individual appearance to one strange to them—just as all negroes look alike to people not used to the race. In this case one could also say, just as all weasels look alike. Not that all trolls are weasels by nature—but that the nature of that blood-sucking cunning animal stared out of these similar, troll faces. The largest of the three men was Red Nake.

Within their little, close-set eyes over the long sharp-ridged noses gleamed no courage and no humanity. Gleamed instead a red glitter of madness—that peculiar madness inherited of some families of the underworld. But in the underworld it is not recognized as madness. Neither did the ancient Norse recognize the "baresarks" as mad, but only as men apt to be seized upon provocation with the lust for bloodshed.

There were three great two-foot-high steps leading up to that seat of forgotten majesty, and also a long ramp for those not equipped with the long legs of the antique men. Upon one of these steps the taller of the three dropped to a seat. He mopped his brow with a red cloth taken from the breast of his armor, for the warm, breezeless air of the caverns is not compatible with the wearing of much covering. The other two continued to divest themselves of the remainder of their armor. Looking up into the red, black-stubbled face of his boss, the seated man waited for the questions he knew were coming. Bonur looked down at him, waiting, too—but also waiting for a signal within his mind from his concealed guard ray-mech and men that the man's words would be checked by the telaug for truth as he spoke. Then Bonur leaned forward saying—

"Well, speak it out. You know what I have waited for a full week—this message you bear me!"

RED NAKE grinned triumphantly, pleased to have kept his master in suspense, and pleased to have a message that was safe to disclose to him. Nake used the antique salutation as is the custom still in the caverns, for Nake believed in formality to those able to harm him.

"My Lord Bonur, the enemy who might have yet unseated us—I mean unseated *you*—is no more a power. His caravan rolled neatly into our circle of war-ray. His ray-finders located not one of our hidden armored rollats before all his gun-pointers died. From the battle I bring you two hundred and fifty captives. One hundred and thirty of these are the women of the House of Pyotyr Flores."

Bonur's eyes appeared from the fat flesh of his red face, glowing and round with the gratifying fulfillment of his plans. He rubbed his heavy ringed hands, covered with bristling black hairs, together.

"Those same women brought about Flore's downfall, my Nake. They would insist on their annual trip to Sable Base. And the weakling would yield to their soft entreaties. Those ancient play-mech of Sable Base, what a friend to me they have been. The women got Flores out of his impregnable home, and onto south Ontal way, where I could lay a neat trap for his return. Full nine years I have built my gins to get that thorn out of my side. Now, he is dead!"

"Not dead, Master. I winged him carefully—myself—in each shoulder. He sits outside at this moment, groaning and waiting your pleasure to groan more loudly."

"Ah Nake—that will *be* a pleasure. A pleasure long awaited!"

Bonur heaved his bulk onto his feet with surprising quickness, descended the three tall ancient steps. He clapped Red Nake on the shoulder, grinning evilly.

"Well done, Nake. For this pleasure you shall be rewarded by the pick of the women you have captured for your own. Now, get Flores in here, like a good fellow—bring him before my eyes!"

Bonur rubbed his hands avidly, continually. The black hairs on the backs of his hands bristled with the same evil anticipation that wreathed his face in gloating smiles. The lurid flowers on the silk of his robe moved in great fluttering movements as he moved—red and green petals rustling softly over the purple field of the silk. He leaned forward, watching the great door through which his enemy would be brought at last to grovel at his feet.

THE double valves of the far door opened again, and through it came Nake, pushing a tall slim figure that staggered and stopped, staggered forward and stopped, to be pushed again. His face was streaked with the tears of desperation and rage, his arms hung useless at his sides, swinging slightly and painfully. Two round burns at each shoulder showed through the charred cloth where the dis-ray had rendered him harmless by burning out his muscles and nerves in his shoulder sockets. He was clothed in a black, tight suit of the old ray-defensive metal weave—a stuff impervious to all but the strongest of ray beams. At neck and at wrists the inner stuff of his shirt, a white-gleaming fabric, overlaid with a pattern of red that showed now mingled oddly with his bloodstains, thrust out in dainty ruffs that were now torn. His shoes were the long upturned points patterned after the medieval styles still affected by some cave peoples.

Flores was a slim, strong man at bay. He stood facing Bonur, his thin, sharp face working in anger that he could strike no blow at the blasphemy he evidently considered the life in the bloated, heavy body of his captor. They stood looking at each other for the space of six breaths, then Flores gritted out—

"Now you have me, you spawn of Hell. Get it over with; there is no room for both of us to live in the same world. Kill me and have done!"

Bonur strode toward the man, stood gloating into his weary, inflamed eyes for a moment, then spat squarely into his face.

"You sniveling scarecrow, already you cry for death. Don't expect death so easily, my fine feathered fool. I have waited too long for the sport to end before it is well started."

Pyotyr Flores took the insult, the red mounted in a rush of blood to his face, then receded as he struggled to control himself. Quieter, he said:

"Bonur, this struggle and piracy among us weakens us all till the first intruder in our holdings will whip us—and you among them. Our people will die under the rays of some mad bunch from the far east or the south—while we roast over their fires. Must we fight thus? Why can't we be at peace and grow strong, as we were when all the ray of the world feared our anger—and no cavern of earth was looted by the wanderers of space. At Sable Base I had much contact with the powerful from many parts of the underworld. They wax mightily insolent to us who once ruled all the western ways from Ontal to Sable Base to Antheria. Our piracy among ourselves in the past ten years will in time cause not only our own fall, but the death of all our peoples. And the ways of the fiercest barbarians of the lost caverns will be the ways of these Eastern caverns, too."

"FLORES, I have heard such bleating before. It is ever the cry of the rebel when brought to bay—let us unite against our mutual enemies. I have no worse enemies on earth than you and yours."

"It is you who have made it so, my 'Lord' Bonur of the Stem. But, ten years ago no black ray from Africa would have cursed me to my face, would have spat upon my shadow—yet that thing I saw and heard and was forced to swallow at Sable Base. And if you went there, worse would happen to you; for you are vastly more hated than ever I have been by the barbarians of the uncivilized caverns. And what would you do about an insult from one of their chieftains with your few hundred cultists—or even if you had time to call together all the mad ones whom you have cultivated—instead of the thousands of swift, sane ray-heads that once answered the banner of the Lord of the Stem-way? Think, Bonur! Me you may kill, but for the sake of men of Ontal and her subject cities, I ask you—think and change your ways. The land is dying under your stewardship. The people of Ontal itself are starving. They cannot earn the prices that are put upon foods. That is because of your taxes, which wring blood from every bit of the necessities of life that passes the Stem toll-posts. Sooner or later they must kill you or die."

"If they cannot pay their debts—there is always the slave block to welcome them. Then they may eat."

"To make the whole peoples of Ontal and the other cities served by the Stem slaves—is that your purpose Bonur, a free man makes a more loyal ray than a slave!"

"Flores, I have more gold than any ruler of the Stem ever had before me. Argue against that!"

"I can! Bonur Golz, I can! There are greater values than gold; there is the spirit of your followers. Yours are hungry for the same gold you hoard. Mine were not so. Yours would every man of them kill you gladly for one small part of that gold, and sometime will! Mine would not so by me. A loyal man at your back cannot be bought with gold. But he can be bought with fair treatment. Can you know that, or are you wholly blind?"

"Words will not save you, Pyotyr Flores. Your death I will have. These soft words will not turn away my ten year-old wrath against you." Bonur twisted his mouth into a savage grin, trying to hold his anger hot against the wise words of this hated man, and failing.

"My Lord Bonur, it is not for myself I try to turn your anger into careful thought. It is for my daughter's sweet sake. Will you give her a car—let her go? She has harmed you in no way. Can you find the mercy in you to do me that one favor?"

Bonur laughed, a hideous laugh that showed in him little of human spirit. A blind lust seemed the soul of him in that laugh, the laugh of a sadist—the laugh of a man who was not truly sane.

"Your daughter, free? Man, you are mad. I shall give her to my things, which I keep on a leash to set against those whom I hate most. You may watch what they do to her over the penetray. You should enjoy their entertainment!"

FLORES had all the time been edging closer to the burly belly of the ruler. At these words he bent and swiftly butted the man with all his strength under the chin. Bonur staggered back and sat down hard on the first great step of the giant's throne, half-unconscious from the blow.

Flores struggled forward awkwardly to kick him, his only weapons his feet, but Nake the Red caught him around the neck with the crook of his elbow and threw him to the floor. Nake struck him several times over the head with his pistol butt and Flores lapsed into stillness, blood from his head staining the polished rock of the floor. Then Nake joined the other two solicitously helping the ruler to his feet.

Bonur shook his head to clear it, then stepped to Flores unconscious body and kicked him hard in the side. The man did not make a sound and Bonur kicked him in the face twice, listening for the sound of bones cracking. Flores' eye, a bloody grape—rolled free. Still he lay unconscious, and Bonur motioned with his hand for the men to take him out.

As they left the ruler mounted the too-high steps laboriously and again sat down on the throne that murder had got him ten years before. He panted, and his face was alternately red, then gray as his heart struggled with his fat to set him to rights again. Somehow the interview had not been the sport he had expected. Well, the fool would pay a thousand times and more for that blow before he died!

Now down onto the gloomy old stone of the throne where he sat came a ray from his watching slave girls, and their trembling voices sought to please him as they stimmed the gross body under the flowered robes. Relaxing under the pleasure of the ancient nerve rays, Bonur thought how they had failed to stop that butt as it was conceived in the mind of the captive Flores—and swore aloud, anger again reddening his face.

"Bring to me that watch-ray who failed to read the mind of the man before me—who failed to protect me as is her duty." Bonur's voice was a panting croak of anger.

THE soft weeping of the fearful girls answered him, for they knew how terrible he was when angered and presently through the doors came the nearly unclad form of his favorite. She was a girl named Sarah Beale. She had been brought to the Stem-palace from the surface as a child, sent down because she had wandered into the warehouse where the trucks were being loaded with goods and supplies. She had been raised under the hands of Bonur's women, and been trained in all the intricate debauchery of strange vices of the ancient pleasure rays since her childhood. Bonur had always had a soft spot in his heart for her. But anger obscured all this in his mind as he looked down upon her. She stood before him weeping, her hair a soft silken aureole of beauty. Her hands clasped fearfully and shyly before her—she stood, not looking up at his face which was an evil mask of hideous anger in the half-light of the huge place.

"If you have anything to say, say it! If you do not think enough of me to save me a blow like that, how do I know you would not do a worse thing, and let a fatal ray beam through upon me some day when we are attacked?"

"Oh, my Lord Bonur, I did not think he could strike you without arms, and I was laughing at some joke the girls were making. It just happened that no one was watching the throne room but myself—all the other rays were watching the far ways for any pursuit or attack that Nake's raid might have occasioned. There are too few of us watchers for all the many ways, the Stem palace needs much more of ray hands than it has, Bonur. Most are far off in their guard duty the last ten days."

"You have deserved death from me, Sarah. But I have a weakness for you, knowing you since you were little. It is your first slip, let it be your last. Bring me the whip!"

The girl went slowly to the place behind the great seat where hung a heavy braided whip of leather, plaited with little bits of metal cunningly set in the thongs. Bending prettily and handing it to him, she bared her back and stood waiting. Bonur rose and brought the whip down twice across her soft young skin, and then looked at the great bloody wheals it had raised quickly upon her back. She had not uttered a cry but stood waiting for the prolonged beating she expected. But Bonur was not the fool some thought him, not always. This girl was an influence with the women of his house, and he did not want them hating him entirely. He cast the whip at her feet and turned away.

"See that a better watch is set hereafter on the throne itself, and double the ray-watch everywhere. Yourself attend to this, or I will know of it and my anger will not be so easily sated. Then tell me who are the people you choose, I may not like them well. See that you do this rightly, my little mouse. Your position in my house is none too certain now."

"Yes, oh lord of my heart." A smile on her sweet face, Sarah picked up the whip. Hanging it in its place, she left. But if Bonur could have seen into her mind, he would have completed the beating till death had claimed her. For Sarah had long hidden her hatred of this thing that was her lord and master.

DOWN in the hidden chambers where only the Satanist's cult and members of Bonur's personal staff were ever admitted—the great truckloads of captives unloaded. Into their cells they were herded, hardly counted. There were but a few dozen armed men about the place, for Bonur did not spend money unnecessarily—and one must pay men who bear arms— slaves are not trusted with weapons. Unfed, they waited out the sleep period, and in the morning came the count and the sentencing. Those who had still some possessions, which they could reveal to Bonur, would live till they were found. The older men whose possessions were entirely in his hands would die. The younger would be sold as slaves in some far city, where they could not find friends to free them against Bonur. The women had a higher price as slaves when they were young as these were. The older women died, too.

And after a long, long time, death came to Pyotyr Flores in those chambers. How it came I will not tell you, but it was time.

Men of the surface think the death camps and slave labor of the world have been wiped out with the fall of the Nazis. But that is not true! They have their smaller counterparts in the vast underworld, and they are far older. The centuries have changed the life of the caverns but little, and that not for the better.

CHAPTER FOUR
Bill and Nita Flores

A FEW miles from the palace of the Stem, in a very lovely chamber of cavern rock, decorated with great sinuous odalisques of the elder races' work, with weird sea plants and other beauties carved in the stone—a girl wife spoke to her husband.

"If the mask that hides our life from the surface were lifted, I am sure our life would be changed. The new influence would sweep away these time-forged cobwebs that bind us so smotheringly—"

Bill Flores' frown was a reflection of the frown that sat on young Nita's white forehead, for it was the frown of people who have looked on Death and managed to elude him so long that very weariness has made him no enemy. It is the frown that honorable men wear when they are under the degrading rule of a despot. Too, they were worried about the non-return of their rich relative and powerful protector, Pyotyr Flores.

"Bonur, the fat tightwad, is too cheap to send out the rays to sweep the cavern ways of bats. The far ways are nearly impassable with bat droppings. The bats themselves are becoming a threat to driving. We are hungry, nothing is done for the people of the city, everything against us. Yet still I think the mask is better on than off, for to remove the ancient mask that hides our life from surface men would result in similar slavery and degradation for all of them."

"But, Bill, when some mad little nomad ray decides it is time to start his epidemic of simulated rheumatic fever—or influenza or whatever—and sets out with his collection of antique junk to simulate all the sensations and ill results of disease—the surface men would know and find some way in time of defending themselves from such silly and devouring persecution. They might even find a way of helping us—there are so many good minds among such a great number of educated people."

"They have nothing with which to fight the antique ray weapons." Bill's frown was ingrained in his forehead as were the problems that caused the frown ingrained in his brain. It had been so in a long line of ancestors who had faced the same problems and failed to find the answer. "Our only hope is a helping visitor from space. Some neighbor world where they have used the ancient secrets openly and developed the use of them benevolently."

"Bill, it is like hoping for God. Men have always hoped for such help, but they do not get it. No one from a planet of sane ray-life will land on this madman's nightmare of a world. And if they did, some ray would see them and find a way of wrecking their ship ere it touched earth."

"Yes, if one landed in New York harbor—and Bonur saw it—he would fire upon it before it had established contact with the surface people to give them weapons that would discover us to them—and give them a chance of defending themselves against us."

"Bill, we have talked of these things so long our very lips know the words, and no thing have we ever found new about them all. It is the same old problem of power in evil hands— power so great that no good men can overcome and obliterate it. We still have the evil degenerates who make our lives miserable with their devilish ways, and they still have the terrific power that even we with all our knowledge of the ancient mech cannot overcome—and there just isn't any answer."

"Well, drop the worry, we are always at it is true."

"I will dance for you, Bill—or with you. For a moment we will forget our misery; even forget we are hungry."

NITA lifted her too-thin, but still beautiful and lithe form from the couch by the telemach screen, and touching a button on an ancient "Lusco" music-mech nearby, poised for a moment while the ancient magic of the God-thought-music thrilled its infinitely varied tones through the rock chamber. Then, picking up the motif of the music with her body's slowly increasing undulations, she swept into a series a dizzying movements that brought the man to his feet in admiration. Then she glided into his arms and the two danced lovingly, gravely, together for a time. Then they flung themselves down upon the couch again, breathless, but not laughing. The man looked at his watch.

"We used to dance for hours, Nita. Now ten minutes tires us. We must get more food, some way. If only Pyotyr would return—if only I could figure where to turn for a hand. We must find a way to live. There is nothing to wait here for, nothing to do! The city itself is starving; food just cannot be got!"

Nita looked at him sidewise, sorrowfully. He read her look.

"No, you beautiful child—you young witch. Not that. I guess we would both rather die."

"But I won't have to do that. I can dance at the 100 Club. The manager knows me; will hire me. And even if the pay will no longer buy food the prices things have become, I can cadge some from the kitchen men for you—and I can get my meals there, and mayhap bring some home."

"It would be the first step, Nita. Sooner or later one of them would see you. They would take a fancy to you, and how could I oppose *them*? It would be the last I would see of you. Better to stay out of sight till Bonur's works have gone the way of all evil things."

"I guess it is better to starve quietly to death, at that." Her smile was tired, but a lovely thing on her too-white face. The red lips drooped like weary flowers over his.

"I think if the surface people knew the Hell we are in, somehow they would find a way to help us."

"Nita, they could not help us. Many of them hate us. They blame us for the mockery, for the vile work of the nomads, and for the proud spite of the evil ones. We would be forced to fight them for our life if they did find a way to struggle against us. Those who do not know us would hate us if they knew the truth of our ancient secret way of hiding the whole wonder of the cavern world from them."

"If the 'Helpers' had a rock borer, they would locate a thin place and bore out to bring in food—without Bonur's tax that starves us all. Can't one be located in the abandoned borings of the old ones?"

"Nita, we have one in readiness, but it is not the time to use it. Even if we were successful, the stool pigeons that wait a chance to get Bonur's stingy favor would squeal on us even as we sold them untaxed food. Even empty bellies will not put spine in some of those worms."

"I know, we have an overabundance of such fools. The whole race of the underworld has lived under such oppression so many centuries, been enslaved and degraded so long they are weak in just those things that would make us free. And the Bosses of the Entrys—and Bonur of our Stem-way—go on choking us to death with taxes."

"The Masked World is a dying world, lately, right enough. But Ontal has declined before in the past and come back again—only after the worst of the Stem gang had died by some brave hand."

BILL bent and absently picked up two magazines, gaudy things with lurid covers. *Exciting* and *Seven-Swank*. He mused aloud. "The taste our panderers show is disgusting, isn't it? Nothing to brag about there, Nita."

"They are horrible. Much of the material is a deliberate, hardly hidden mockery of all of us who are out of power, out of favor with the inner gang. A mockery of all the underdogs. The pictures are scenes of torture and death of sometimes well known figures of our life—thinly disguised—to appear like posed scenes. But in reality everyone knows it is the evil rule bragging of its power by showing its secret torture chambers off to us. It is supposed to strike fear into us to keep us from thinking of resisting the death that eats at us all."

"They are horrible, right. They seem to be published for sadists and mindless fools. Look at this scene in *Exciting;* those girls tortured with hot chains. I have seen such things and I swear these are genuine scenes of actual torture."

Nita pointed to a girl in the picture. "See, her back bleeds from a dozen wounds that are incompletely retouched. Those long scars show on her back from previous beatings. Now she is plainly dying of the hot chains. There is no end to our degradation. We are supposed to buy and enjoy these scenes of our bravest and best being tortured to death."

"It was a sad day for Ontal when Bonur seized the palace of the Stem, and set his taxes on our only food source."

"I think his real idea is to reduce us all to slaves. When the people get hungry enough, they will seek the auction block, to get the food for themselves and the money for their people to buy food. When the strength of the city and of the neighboring cities that feed from the Stem-way is gone, Bonur need have fear of no one."

"The *Seven-Swank* magazine has an article saying—'The Control Arsenals, built so long ago by the mighty Elder race, will outlast the race. The power output is undiminished, time affects the machinery not at all and much of the machinery is in complete repair.'" Nita sighed.

"In other words there is no hope for the people. I think the article is a lot of lies. While the ancient power-mech does not deteriorate visibly, a strange force comes from the old machines the more they are used. Something is changed in them by use and time. The older they are in use, the less do the machine tenders and mechanics like to approach them. There are emanations from the most-used old power-mech that cause serious burns to anyone near them too long, and the power— the electric from them—once beneficial and good when used in the ben-ray mech, now causes the same ben-ray mech to give off only detrimental rays. The article is an attempt to cover the spread of such information; to make themselves feel safe. There is plenty of anger ready and waiting to blast at them the first opportunity—and the power arsenals are becoming a weakness instead of a strength."

"But what sort of opportunity does that give us? No underdogs ever yet overcame the powerhouses or the central control arsenals before."

"I have often thought that a poisoner's club might give us the answer. I can't figure how to work the poisoning with the constant watch by the rodite over the telaug beams. Can you, Nita, figure how it might be done?"

"Only if the rodite were in on the plot. I fear even to think of the idea when I know they may be watching and reading my thought."

"Old Benz is one of the rodite clique, and an old one among them. He might be able to swing it for us. He must know what cruel idiots this bunch around Bonur are—what they do to us."

"Bill, no! If you talk to him, sound him out very carefully; he might have to turn on you if he thought you had talked the idea over with others—were foolishly careless. He might be in the confidence of Bonur, anything might happen. If only Uncle Pyotyr would return…"

"We've got to do something, Nita. I will try to bum some money off of Benz, and if it looks favorable, I will discuss the poison idea as someone else's idea I had heard. Then if he is favorable I will suggest our working it out. He may be able to get me some food at the very least."

ABOVE the despairing lovers roared the traffic of New York, but unheard by them through the miles of rock. For they were citizens of the Masked World, and New York does not form a part of that world—except as a port of entry for the favored few. The lower classes—whom Nita had recently joined because of the inadequacy of their income due to the taxes—never go in or out of the "Stem" of their world.

Bill got up and went out, after kissing Nita a fond goodbye. He did not need a hat, or a coat, for the temperature of the caverns never varies from a warm dry heat that its people are habituated to.

As Bill passed one of the great windows set in the houses of the "Elder" world, he heard a conversation—for the windows of the cavern world have no need of glass, are chiefly placed for ventilation—revealing to him the hopeless condition of law in the formerly endurable city.

"Do you know what you have signed? I will tell you, you fool. You have signed a power of attorney, which gives me full control of your money, your houses, all your possessions. You see, I do not have to marry you to get what I want from you! We of the Wast's get what we want without debasing ourselves."

Bill looked into the luxurious lounge of the great home. On a divan sprawled a slightly gowned, tigerish young beauty whose well-fed form told Bill she was one of those close to Bonur. She was laughing sneeringly at a slender young man before her, who stood with a pen in his hand staring down at a document he had just signed. Bill knew what had made him sign it, for in the rear of the room another woman was holding a ray-beam upon the helpless man while she waited. It was a synthetic "will" ray of a pleasant nature that Bill could feel even outside. Bill knew the man had been controlled by the ray from the ancient ro-mech, had had no choice but to do what the operator willed him to do with the mechanism's strong beam. Bill hurried on, fearing to be seen listening, but could not help hearing the rest of the words...

"You she-devil!"

The woman's nasty, triumphant laughter answered.

"You will tell no one and do nothing about this for you are going into our special little room where we keep fellows like you on ice till we need them for some rigmarole or other that our laws require. Then you will appear, under control, and the formality will be observed. When we are through with you— you know how you will die."

Bill knew how the man would die, too. He knew the habits of the sadists. Sadism was fashionable; for the ruling clique being so inclined, everyone who toadied and expected to get along with the gang in the palace of the Stem affected cruelty as a character, to be in line with the ruler. The poor slaves and other victims suffered the whip daily, and regularly many helpless men and women died in various strange and intricate ways—ways which the slaves spent much time in devising and executing in order to escape a similar fate themselves. And everyone who was "in" watched such parties of blood and death and feigned to enjoy it all very much, because not to do so would be to be marked by the spies as a potential enemy of the great Bonur and his cronies.

FURTHER down the way—called the "Street of the Sleepers," after the great statues with closed eyes which lined the way—Bill passed a young girl in a doorway, weeping and wiping something from her shapely bare legs—wiping something that on closer look proved to be spattered blood.

"What happened, did you hurt yourself?" asked Bill. The girl glanced up at him and sobbed out—"Oh, my mistress whipped me! I can't stand it, I can't! And every week it's the same, for their fun…"

Bill had seen such parties among the sadists himself and knew what she meant. So he finished her speech for her— "And if you run away—you would be caught, and then you would be killed! I know, Ontal is in the worst shape I have ever seen it—or heard of."

As Bill went on his way helplessly, he knew that sooner or later the young slave-girl's white body would grace the entertainment with its dying torments.

Ever about Bill as he passed the poorer quarters people begged of him for a coin to buy a bit of food. Bill pitied them and showed them his empty hands and went on.

And Bill went into the offices of the "rodite" who are the police of Ontal—for rodite is the ancient's word for police, and he passed in his card with a note asking to be brought before the chief of this section, Rudy Benz. Benz was old in the service and possessed of some influence, which he might turn to account.

Inside, Rudolph Benz, the old Rodite chief noted the young man's approach sadly. He knew the young fellow was on the proscribed list since his uncle, Pyotyr Flores, had been taken by Bonur Golz' henchmen. He would certainly have to arrest him! And very few survived the prisons for long nowadays; there was little food for even a free man in the city. Especially would one of Flores' line be sure to die, for Bonur hated the family as well as wanted no heirs about to dispute his confiscation of the wealth.

Rudolph Benz looked down and smiled sadly on William Flores from his high desk. They were old acquaintances, but Benz ignored this as well as the card bearing his name, which Bill had sent in.

"You are James Bean, aren't you? Can you tell me what brings you here?"

Bill, slow on the uptake, as well as being hampered mentally by a vengeful watch-ray interfering with his thought, did not understand Benz' subterfuge or the reason for it. Why should Benz affect not to recognize him—to mistake him for someone else?

"Chief, you know me as well as you know your own son. I am William Flores, of this city." Bill's words came as a surprise to himself, and he realized that the watch ray had made him speak by control in order to get him into some trouble, which Old Benz was trying to keep him from.

An obsequious clerk, lifting his head from his many scribblings, saw and sensed exactly what was going on. He got up and bustled over to Benz, his beady eyes and unhealthy face alight with the opportunity to check the old man in an error. His short but loudly whispered "All Flores' men are ordered held by Lord Bonur," Bill could was unable to hear fully, but he was able to see by Benz' face that it probably meant some disaster to him.

Benz realized it was no use trying to shield Bill Flores, for his clerk would squeal on him. So he said sorrowfully, "William Flores, it is my solemn duty to arrest you in the name of the law. Your uncle, Pyotyr Flores, has been adjudged guilty of treason, and all his friends and relatives and persons otherwise associated with him are suspects—to be held for examination. Officers, do your duty!"

Bill turned, desperately seeking with his eyes for a non-existent way of avoiding the trap he had so trustingly walked into. Even as he turned, two burly coppers in the gray tunics of Bonur's police seized his arms. Bill struggled wildly, crying out to Benz.

"My goodness, Benz, if I knew anything about it at all, would I have walked in here with my both of my eyes open? I wanted to see you on a personal matter, as well as to ask you if you had recently heard any news of my uncle, who has been in Sable Base for approximately two months. This is all a fearful mistake."

The clerk, a thin lipped smile of satisfaction at having the whip hand over Benz for a moment, spoke loudly.

"The examination will certainly bring out his innocence or guilt. He is under suspicion, and we must above all obey orders."

Old Benz said nothing, only smiling sadly at Bill, resolving in his mind to "get something" on that double-damned clerk if it was the last thing he ever did. For everyone in the room knew that few men survived a police "examination" when they were heirs to a fortune, as Bill was since Flores was under sentence of death. Bonur would see to that, for even in the little-regarded law books, the state took over all such moneys that had no claimants.

CHAPTER FIVE
To Find a Poison

"MURDER doesn't matter, down here!"

The speaker was a long-nosed man of a wizened, wise face and peculiar, gnarled and gnomish appearance. His blood was different from others in the city, being from the Picts of the Northlands of England, while mostly the other ray people of Ontal were from southern and western Europe, of nearly the same build and appearance as modern Americans, though the ages of their ancestors life in the caverns gave them a lighter, less-muscled build, lighter bones, and the extremely white skin of all the cavern people. There were other differences from surface man—larger eyes, and in this man a bigger, almost grotesque mouth; and a quicker, more alert look in the eyes. His name was Brack Longen, and he was bending over Nita. Her nearly dead young body had been found by him, fearfully emaciated, waiting silently for the return of her man, or for death.

"Get some milk, and warm it at the heat place…" Brack spoke sharply to his companion Tim Shanter. "We don't want our old friend Nita to die."

Tim hastened about his task, but found no milk in the place. He brought some water from the great flowing dragon mouth of the ancient fountain in the center of the room and warmed it for a moment over the electric heat rods of the heat-place, then put it to Nita's lips tenderly.

"Child, why didn't you call us? What do you think friends are for? We can get food where children like you and Bill fail. And what has become of Bill?"

Nita looked up at him mutely, then gathering her strength—

"Brack, I know he is dead—and I did not want to live without him. Why did you have to come? As soon as I heard Pyotyr Flores had been taken by Bonur, I knew what had become of Bill."

"Ah, nonsense, child. He is probably well and waiting at the prison pens for you—and sore as a boil you haven't been to search for him. Now get your backbone stiffened!"

SOME hours later, after Brack and Tim had gotten some liquid food into Nita's system, they carried her out to their waiting rollat and carefully placed her in the great seat in the back, a seat built to hold the enormous bodies of the ancient race. There are modern trucks and cars from the surface in use but still the antique vehicles are used, for they are superior, faster, and more dependable. But they get rarer as times goes on.

Brack's voice was quite bitter. "Murder really doesn't matter, nor any other rotten thing, since Bonur got hold of the Stem. At one time we of the underworld had some defense against evil. But those days have gone. No way of getting food but to do Bonur's bidding, and so we starve and die—as Nita nearly has."

Tim looked at Brack's long-nosed, thin face. It was the face of a bitter, over-wise gnome, but the spirit that is MAN moved behind it.

"Brack, how are you able to conceal these kinds of thoughts from the rodite-ray? We will be seized, if you let yourself go so."

Brack looked at Tim wryly. "There is simply no way to keep from thinking, and so long as these evils go on, such as you and I must give our lives attempting to keep from being noticed as rebellious thinkers. We would leave Ontal for good, if we were wise. But you know why we stay. We know of no place that is better, for the mad rays devil all men in the unsettled places, and it is certain death to venture out into that uncharted, endless labyrinth."

"Brack, I went to the circus yesterday. Lura the dancer died. You remember her; the beauty of her was in every heart that ever saw her. The great ones commanded her, but by subtle means she kept her body's freedom so she could dance for all of us. They commanded her to their homes sometimes, but, strangely, after some months or weeks—those whom Lura had entertained unwilling, the most cruel of our powerful men, died of some strange sickness. A dozen of them she killed before they got their heads together and connected her with the deaths. Some subtle poison of old she slipped into their veins in their sleep…and went sweetly on her way. From that day they sickened slowly and died. At last the fire claimed her in the circus, but I swear the stim-rays followed her every pain and quenched it ere it hurt her. Such as her have always friends among the ray-peoples. Her death was not really painful, she smiled upward as if in ecstasy as the flames consumed her, not a quiver or a pitiful scream from her did they get to gloat over.**

"And she relieved us of a dozen oppressors…"

Brack held up a hand.

"Tim Shanter, you have given me an idea! Say no more of this till we have reached our metal room." Brack's lips twisted over the rotted teeth—teeth that Brack knew were rotten because there was no food to keep teeth whole available to him. Brack was not pretty, but Brack was a man.

**Under our feet the Masked World goes on it's evil consuming way. The future of all men is squandered there in endless orgies whose nature no surface man can comprehend—for words will not tell of the pleasures of stim-death, of the pleasures of sadism made infinitely more so by augmentation of all the body's and mind's impulses. And likewise for the torments of the victim—they are made infinitely more painful by augmentation of all the body's nerve messages.

That future that they squander is the minds of men able to understand the uncorroded machines that are their ancient power—able to understand the necessity for study of the ancient lore that abounds still in the endless labyrinths of the Masked World. For the area of Masked World is greater by far than the surface area of Earth for the dense stone of the deep caves keeps out even the slightest trace of dampness from miles of sea even overhead. And there are as many levels to the greatest old buildings of the ancients within the rock of the underworld as there are floors to a skyscraper—and more beside, for if their is one thing noticed down there it is that there is always more passages, more levels above and below, more and more endlessly of the ancient city that covered the whole world deep under the surface.

Multiply the floor area of a skyscraper by the area of the U.S. and you may get some idea of the immense and largely unexplored area of the Elder World.

It is a world that the rulers of the few existent entries keep choked of all development because they fear all intelligent growth, for they are deficient. Those rays lying about unused everywhere about the endless corridors of dense, unyielding rock…anyone of those ancient mechanisms would revolutionize all surface science; but the rulers of the Masked World are too devilishly mean to give the surface man even one tiny bit of that ancient science for study, one bit of that endlessly intricate mech for analysis.

That is fear of what we may do with it—and a thing as craven as that is not worthy of our fear. I say to you who fear these worm-like spirits who keep these things from us—those non-existent souls of the more evil of those below—fear them not, and bring about what we know must be brought about before man can advance into his future.—Author.

THE mysterious "Helpers" of the underworld are descendants of those families among them who have always, according to legend and tale, helped man by doing him favors that man has considered only a "God" could do. These "Helpers" are still a force in the underworld, which guards always such men as Tim and Brack. These "Helpers" of the underworld guard me as I write. For the evil of the Masked World are of reputation and fact loath to be exposed to the eyes of those men whom they have injured so terribly and so continually since the earliest times.

As Tim and Brack stepped from the old rollat at their destination—the helpers found their work necessary. A telesolidograph projection of sudden struggle sprang into existence about the two men. Tim and Brack, old hands at evasion of the far eye of a nosy police ray, dropped to the pavement so that the images of the solidograph might take their places upon the far screens of the police rays' mech. And in that twinkling as they dropped, the clever hands of the helpers substituted projection for flesh where Tim and Brack had stood. It was a "fake" attack by the Helpers, Tim and Brack knew from past experience, planned to supplant a real attack by bonafide police under Bonur.

Brack and Tim crawled rapidly away from the scene, and allowed a half hour to elapse before they returned for the sleeping Nita. The sudden struggle about them of the solid-seeming projection of men and weapons they knew was a warning as well as a saving device. The rodite police of Bonur must know somewhat of their activities and have set a watch ray upon their home, and the Helpers must have lied to the "watchers" saying that they themselves planned to obliterate the two men. All this they knew instantly by deduction and by past experience with the methods of the Helpers. They had no great respect for Bonur's rodite, for the "Helpers" often foiled their distant watch ray with such image devices and many another trick that is better not set down here for still in use.

But the incident had the further value of telling them they were "looked for," "wanted" men—and they knew the scene had saved their lives by throwing the real pursuit off the trail. The corrupt, hereditarily lazy ray-watch would drop their watch after seeing them so providentially disposed of by parties unknown or fictitious in some secret "Helpers" report. Nor if they turned up living later would much be said—for the ray watch were a lazy lot as were most of Bonur's parasitic bunch who tended to nothing so much as their own safety and comfort, and acted only on direct pressure from Bonur or his inner clique.*

WHAT the watch ray saw from the distance was a projection of a car roll up beside Tim and Brack's rollat, stop and fire on the two men. They saw the two men get out, fall to the pavement, saw the attackers also get out, approach the two bodies, kick them, pick them up and throw them in the car and drive off, leaving the corroded old rollat stand where it was. That none of this happened they did not know, for at a distance none could say whether a telesolidograph projection was real or unreal. They were fooled, and it saved them from going after the two themselves. Any exertion on their part was a thing to be put off as long as possible. In that they were not unlike surface police, though perhaps more so due to hereditary laziness. Tim and Brack held their minds blank for the benefit of anyone watching now and trusted to the unknown friendly ray to keep the danger from them. Their steps hastened again to their parked rollat and their wheels sped now toward another destination more likely to prove safe than this. They were going

---

*Indeed, the slothfulness of upper-class members of the underworld is proverbial. They lie about all day long, slaves spoon the food into their mouths, remove their offal, and wash them! Dreams from the dream-mech, stimulating pleasure rays from the stim-mech, are their life! It is their sloth that is responsible for the horrible conditions in some of the underworld's biggest peopled areas. They have the power to correct, will not do so—nor let others do so.—Author.

to a friend, a very wise friend of theirs, whose name was Ben Uniaty.

The ancients equipped certain rooms in the vast warrens with a metal lining impervious to detrimental rays (to serve the same purpose as our air raid shelters)—a dense stuff of awful weight—and to the unaided eye these rooms much resembled others lined with other kinds of metal. If one were wise to the ways of the ancients one soon knew which were "metal rooms" and which were not. Tim and Brack had long made use of one of these special rooms for their hangout, and its impervious secrecy had long protected them from all police ray charges of rebellious thoughts. Likewise had old Ben Uniaty built himself a great laboratory, little by little through the years, where no watch ray ever disturbed his thought. When they left these rooms they made up their mind as one makes up a bed; to the eye of the mind reading telaug rays they were people completely in love with their miserable condition and their worthless, cruel oppressive overlords. Once home again they could relax and curse them, or plot to their heart's content, which gave them much satisfaction, though little had come of it so far in truth.

Within the secret walls, they had stored many tools of their trade. Likewise in Ben Uniaty's huge burrow deep under Ontal they had made a practice of storing all the strange or broken mech they had been able to pick up through the years of their work around the great, half-empty city. For their trade was repair work on the ancient, intricate mech, and that trade is a hereditary one in the Masked World. They had also many weapons and similar forbidden things, which could be explained if they should have to as things given them for repair. But the necessity for such explanation was seldom required due to the aforesaid sloth of the watchers. Their trade was one favored highly over all others, for the need for such work was very great, and they were in truth privileged characters of the city.

INSIDE the great, laboratory-like place, they saw no signs of old Ben Uniaty. But the place was big as an office building, with many rooms, and Ben might be at work anywhere about on some of his own mysterious experiments. Brack made Nita comfortable and turned to Tim.

"Tim Shanter, remember I said to you that you had given me an idea?"

"Aye, Brack, I remember well, I have been wondering what it was that caught your mind so?"

"Tim, the cooks—the under-cooks of Bonur's staff—are slaves of little mind. They are those 'cut' of brain in their childhood to make them as tractable to work without pay as possible. They cannot reason, cannot remember well, know little outside of their daily work. If we could give them some of Lura's fatal poison as a seasoning—something they would not know was poison—the watch-ray would never read the danger in their minds."

"Brack, many of our best protectors, even some of the unknown 'Helpers,' dine at the banquets of the evil ones we hate so. They would die too?"

"There are certain gatherings to which the good are neither admitted nor would they attend. It is those feasts where girls die under the super-stim for the entertainment, where those men like ourselves burn all night in the pain-fires to light their feast—those feasts where all the evil we know secretly exists is openly displayed. The flesh of a babe is the sacred wafer, and the whole evil throng worships the image of Satan—an image that comes to life and takes part in the orgies, so they say. Some of that human flesh they eat then could be the bearer of the poison that would free us at one blow."

"You mean the Feast of the Sabbath, though there are other feasts of the Devil cult that would do as well. But the Sabbath—ah, for that they have been gathering from places no man knows the name for—even from Panama and beyond in the caverns of South America they have come to the Sabbath of Ontal, for it is famous among them all. The city is full of strange wild cultists from everywhere the name of Ontal has become known. If we got the poison into that feast it would surely do the life of the whole cavern world more good than by any other trick we could pull."

"Well, Tim, that is my idea, and the first step is a risky bit of work for which you are better fitted than myself. If you get stuck with it, it will mean the death of all of us and no mistake. But it must be done!"

"I'll manage it, Brack, tell me."

"You know what my thought-concealer is and why we keep it in reserve so the coppers are not on to its use. Since there are so few records suitable for such a small reader as is in this headpiece there are few who would understand what my invention was if they saw it."

"What is the job, Brack, and why wear the concealer? We do well enough ordinarily without it."

"Because I'm sending you to Lura's place to get the mysterious poison she used, before the lazy coppers get around to searching the place thoroughly. You know how thick-headed Bonur's cops are, and it may be they never got it through them that Lura really had a poison, or never understood it must be hidden somewhere in her rooms. If we can get to the stuff we may be able to wipe out all the men who make our lives miserable with one use of it, instead of many trips to the well, as Lura used it."

"I get your idea, Brack. You want me to wear your thought record of me doing some work on Lura's mech, as if I didn't know she were dead and were doing something she ordered before she died—diddle-daddle with her sewing machine or what-have-you, and come back with the poison."

"I'LL watch you all the time from our metal room and I'll be able to stave off any trouble you might get into. It is a big risk, for the coppers might just have 'left' the stuff there as a trap to catch anybody who happens to get the idea I have. But I'm gambling our lives on the chance that the cops never proved that Lura had a poison, that the deaths were anything but accident, and that the big-shots had Lura killed just in case.

With their usual stupidity, they should be leaving Lura's place unguarded and deserted. The only reason I'm taking such a gamble is that I never heard of a poison as untraceable, as long in its suspended action, as potent in small doses as the one Lura used. Why, some of her victims died two months after Lura got it to them! That gives us plenty of time to get out of the city after the big feast next week. So, if there is anybody around when you get there, pretend Lura ordered you to fix her stim-mech or something, and that you haven't heard that she died yesterday."

"O.K., Pal! I don't see any great danger in the job. We have pulled worse stunts."

"Tim, the danger lies in that some of the powerful friends of those who died at Lura's hands may be wise to her method, and be using her place as a trap for others of like mind. Bonur himself may be watching the place from a ray on the Stem. How do we know?"

"I'll bring back anything that looks like it might be a poison—her face powder, her perfume, and if there are any around, some of her photos and maybe a statuette! I've heard of some that are the nuts."

"Never mind the bric-a-brac, Tim; get the poison, and if everything goes all right, Bonur will be pushing up daisies inside a month. That is worth the effort and risk, Tim. It is doubtful if the thieves have dared to enter to loot as yet. I suspect that even the police would not like to be caught there by certain people if they suspect the truth of the deaths that followed Lura's loves. The big-shots may be looking for the poison. You're taking a big risk, and don't forget it for a minute! And on second thought, Tim, bring me a photo of her—dancing— the way she used to be when things were well with her. I want it for my personal collection."

"No bric-a-brac, eh, Brack! I'll bring anything that will keep her memory alive—the woman who dared do what the men of Ontal failed to do."

"Get going, Tim! You may be covered by the Helpers, or by some friend of ours, as well as myself from here. Get going, man!"

DOWN the dark, blue-lit ways traveled the old rollat which Tim and Brack had resurrected from Ontal's dump long before. Rollats were almost numerous, but one could not buy them—most antique mech, which is still in working condition, is hard to come by for several obvious reasons. It just isn't built any more. But such men as Tim and Brack were sometimes in possession of immensely valuable samples of the old machine art because of their knowledge, their ability to repair such intricate devices as the ancients constructed—where richer men were not able to acquire them.

Past the marvels of marble known as the "Sea People's Fountain," where the mermen stretched their flippers endlessly over the arcing water sprays of the fountain of the ancient allied race of the sea—with their name that looked like "Mistmen" carved in the antique letters still discernible in the ancient stone. Past the great statue of the Goddess of Sleep, of blue transparent stone that sparkled inwardly with mysterious fires like stars set in the night sky, stone that was shaped into a gigantic and exquisite woman who seemed to strew sleep over the city with her great graceful hands.

Over the Bridge of the Dead; past the glittering yellow stone of the palace of the forgotten Queen Hynay the Golden; past the tremendous green faces of the "Square of the Kings" where the terrible wisdom carved into the visages of the ancient rulers of Bakt looked out over the whole vast bowl of Ontal: the awful deeps of character engraved in their faces was a thing that never failed to thrill and shiver the soul of the passer-on rolled the ancient conveyance, its indestructible atomic motor purring as sweetly as ever it did in the past when it was born of the clever hands of the God-like men of forgotten ancient time.

Up to the "Place of the Hetaerae" as the building was still called, and for which the place was still used, where Lura had been one of the beauties there quartered. For all the high-class entertainers and dancers were made to live in this tremendous edifice where they might be handy to the wants of the "powers that be."

THE rollat purred to a halt in the darkness of the passage between the Place of the Hetaerae and the "Home of the Blinded." In the dark gloom cast by the shadow of the gloomy old "Home" (for even the workers of that far past had their accidents sooner or later in the endless lives their medicinal science gave them so that the legend of their immortality still is remembered today), Tim parked the rollat in the shadow of the overhanging stone monster of stone that graced the weird architecture of the great pile. Grabbing his bag of tools, Tim Shanter scuttled across the dim alley cavern into the dark doorway, up the slim winding stairs that led to the service doors of the rich hetaerae. A couple of revelers passed him on the stairs, with ribald references to his dirty clothes, drunkenly thinking him one of themselves seeking the favors of some beauty who sold her charms. Up to the top that was not the top, *for no building of the ancients ceases to ascend up and up into the rock within the limitations of one man's strength.* Up to the door marked Lura 198—and tried the door with a shaking hand.

Fear gripped Tim and the humming inside his head from Brack's thought-concealer only heightened his fear. Its obscuring thought impulses added to his own its constant reminder of his danger. But nothing alarmed him as the door swung open under his hands manipulating the set of picklocks he knew well how to use. He let himself into the apartment of the sweet beguiler and poisoner of the worst of the evil men of the city—Lura—perhaps the greatest figure, and surely the greatest dancer, of her time in all Ontal.

Sweet she looked down from her statue, life colored, poised above the fire rods of the heat place. Sweet, yes—but much more: the artist had caught the idealistic flame that was the life in Lura, the sheer courage that animated every line of her, the utter cunning that had made her able to do what she had for the oppressed of Ontal. On the walls were several paintings of her. Tim knew she had probably paid some needy artist lavishly for them, for she was noted for her generosity. And Tim imagined the artist refusing the needed money, for she was well loved by all who knew her well.

Soft were the hangings that glittered iridescent over the walls. Her bed—a great sculptured couch of the ancients, not a cheap work bought in modern times—flashed with a million of the tiny, magical "sleep-stones" that gave off the subtle rays from reflected light that can give sleep to the most restless, do they gaze at them a short while.

The bed was carved antelopes couchant, holding their horns upright for the four posts that drooped downward a curtain of soft fire—the fabric called Cammetta—that is ever scented with some fabulous forgotten magic odor that makes a man want woman more than life. And embroidered over the shifting fire of the fabric were many queer flowers and poppy's and little forgotten beasts of strange unknown kinds sleeping among them—and other sleepy dreams from some artist's time-vanished hand.

All this was pain to Tim, for his starved soul relished such beauty as a man on a desert relishes the oasis, and it was sheer pain to have to disregard all the beauty and hasten about his job. He had no time for the beauty, which Lura had so loved and had given her life to protect and help to grow again in the lives of men.

QUICKLY Tim set about pulling open closets, feeling with his quick fingers for false drawers, and levers that might open secret panels; meanwhile he swung open the rhythm-tone mech that sat at the bedside and set it going. It was a device that changed the basic rhythm at which it was set into a number of subtly developing variations—a kind of automatic composer of simple dance rhythms of a varied kind that Lura had used in her dancing practice. Now he had an excuse for being there; he could say he was repairing this device as Lura had ordered.

Into his bags went the powders, the perfumes, the whole contents of her cabinets of beauty aids, and as his eyes sought quickly over the room for what could not be what he sought in order to search more closely that which might contain it, his eye fell on her vita-wood desk where her feather-pen stood in its dragon ink-well, trailing a peacock feather aloft as the dragon's tail.

Under the desk his intuitive fingers found a bump where no bump should be, and he pressed. His hands felt a tiny door open under the apparently solid wood of the desk. His eyes searched the outer doors of the apartment fearfully, for now was one moment he would not want to explain to any who might catch him there, for he knew he had found what he sought.

His ears listened, and every faint sound from the huge building full of revelry and far-off muffled whispers and secretive comings and goings seemed the step of the men he feared, the men who obeyed Bonur's least wish (and for whom they would skin the flesh from a man transparent slice by slice). But the silence was real, and his fear left him.

Within the place his fingers had opened stood a round bag full of something, and his heart skipped a beat for it had an odor that spoke death in no uncertain language. It must be very potent, for the very odor of the stuff made him faint and dizzy. Only a little would betray itself instantly, but perhaps she disguised it with some strong perfume mixed in.

He had what he wanted, so he switched off the rhythm-tone, and stole down the stairs that were the way trod by those whom the hetaerae loved but dared not let be seen enter the front ways for fear of the men who paid their bills. Sometimes the very best blood of the city worshipped here at the shrine so many men have burned their souls before. And well they might, for the ages of evil in Ontal, the centuries just past, and the centuries of life of the people where they had come to enter the caverns of America—had seen the breeding of slave-women for beauty as horses are bred—to a beauty surpassing the normal of downtrodden Ontal by far. It was of these that

Lura was, but dancers are exempt from compulsion to other forms of diversion, except by those who are powerful enough to flout all restrictions and command her.

NOW down and down Tim went, and ever in his ears the clever device of Brack's kept whispering silly nothings—of the delights of hitting a pool ball dead center and seeing the target take its pocket; of swimming in the life-fountain and losing the rheumatism in its strangely vitalized water from the old water-making machine underneath; of going to the circus and seeing the bad criminals be slaughtered and burned and otherwise done away with. And never a whisper in the thought that poured through his head of the fact that the criminals it spoke of were the best blood and brains of the city, men who hated the evil that swallowed all of life enough to fight for them—and got caught at it—and nothing in his thought of his own rage at the misery and crumbs of life that were left him from the destroying rich.

And the mirrors on the landings of the many stairs leered his face back at him with its pall of fear, his face that was bright red when he was happy, but had not been so for years now.

He tossed the bags in the back of the big rollat and got into the driver's place. Lifting the seat he tucked the poisonous-odorous bag into the place where tools would be if there were tools any more to fit the rollat. Over it he spread his coat and onto the ragged coat he flung some tools: the heavy pipe wrench and a stack of tiny pliers and wrenches for the delicate telaug repair work.

Well, he was safe enough, though he had forgotten to garner many of the jewels that were flung carelessly about Lura's rooms, the emeralds that had swung at her neck, at her navel and at her G-string in the dance of Green Fire; the sapphires of yellow that had blazed at her waist in a wide belt in the "Flame" dance; the ancient priceless jewels given her by the Lord of the Entry long ago that could not possibly be used to cover her at all, but were for her head, her soft column of neck, her wrists and ankles only. Two great old jewels he had picked up with the perfumes from her cabinets and then the things had slipped his mind in the excitement of searching for a hidden place among all the delicate priceless furniture of the favorite dancer's home.

As he swung the old rollat back on the deserted Ontal-way again and headed for the metal room where Brack waited and chewed his stubs of finger nails in Ben Uniaty's lab, he thought with hate of the Lords of the Entry who could order any dancer or woman to dance the most shameless dances and endure the most revolting degradations while those same Lords closed the dance halls to the people if even a little bare skin were shown, who pretended to deplore the trend toward vulgarity although it had been always the way of the underworld to be shameless and pagan in its pleasures—till the later time of the ruler before Bonur who had hypocritically condemned all pleasure on the grounds of vulgarity, but in truth purely through a desire to be cruel. And how at first they had been glad when Bonur had killed him and taken the Stem for his own, but they had learned differently.

Tim boiled still as he remembered the smug way the powerful ones laughed at the people who might not ever enjoy the beauty of the dancers or see the hetaerae or any beauty of any kind but must only be allowed to see them as they died. And now that was worse than the one before Bonur. For, just as Lura had died in the flames of the stake at the circus for the entertainment of the people who had loved her and known her heart was good, so had others they loved best. And he thought of the ancient Palace of Love of the old ones that had been a theatre for so many years down here—why once even the Indians had used the Palace of Love for a temple to their great spirit—and here the sachems had come secretly to worship at the shrine of the ancients. And when the white men had come they had kept the secret from him, but the men of the underworld of Europe had come too and had driven them at last from this hiding place as well.

NITA had danced there before Bill had met and loved her, and he recalled how he himself had loved Nita, though he had never told her, and had spent all his money going night after night to see her dance—and how the Lords had closed the ancient Palace of Love because the dances were lewd, and the ancient statuary "too frank" in its exposition of the nature of animal love, of spiritual love, and genuine love. While all the time they had done the thing only to deprive the people of the things they liked best themselves so that they could point to a pleasureless people and say to their sycophants, "There, but for my favor, goes yourself: without pleasure and without dance or the sight of woman to gladden your eyes; without love songs or any erotic relief from dull living; without the dream-maker's beauties to gladden you—be faithful and spiritless and you will not have to join them, but work against me and you will become one of the spiritless workers."

As Tim drove the hate grew in his breast and he growled. Most of all he hated the hypocritical phrases they put upon such deeds as "virtue winning over the ancient vice"—that the dances of the underworld, so old as to be ritual, so frankly worshipping of Astarte and Aphrodite to be not lewd but spiritual, was the worst insult of all. And he wondered if the surface men were so evil in their so-called goodness and he wished that they were not. For he saw their newspapers sometimes and knew their leaders were often guilty of the same hypocrisy of forbidding the people what they loved themselves, while they raided those lesser places where the lesser people indulged.

But Tim did not know that evil is a repetition ever, and makes the same pattern wherever it goes, in great or less degree, yet the same. But Tim knew that though it did not seem so, the worst evil these evil ones did to the people was to kill their pleasure and make their life too dull to bear.

As he turned the corner past that long-vacant palace of the ancient worship of the goddess of Love, he thought of the priceless stim apparatus that stood beside the antelope bed of Lura, and knew that it must be the gift of some light-fingered one from among the rich class—for stim was forbidden everywhere except in the homes of the very rich and powerful. Such as Lura could only get it by paying most of their "take" to the stim monopoly, who had taken most of the stim mech's antique magic and stored it in vaults. Tim realized that Lura had been far from friendless to be so privileged as to have a jewel encrusted stim-mech beside her bed, for such privileges were won by few. Who had taken it from the vaults for her but one of those who guard the vaults from the many who would die for a taste of the forbidden pleasures?

Tim thought back of the time when the love palace was every man's right, and the right of the women who had made of love a religion and a heaven, and of the stim that had been the right of anyone who could press a button and activate the ancient mech that sat everywhere about the city just where the ancients had left it when they went away so long ago. Tim groaned to think of all the present rulers had taken from him and his kind. Once life had been full and rich, now it was empty.

TIM passed the fountains of sleep and drew up before the terrible tower of dread that was the building above the deep chambers where Uniaty had made his home and where Brack waited in the metal rooms that lay deep within. Tim wondered what that black round tower of solid stone had been so long ago that it still should strike such eerie dread to the sense. He entered and wound his way down to the place where Brack waited and pondered how to cause the death of those whom they all hated.

"Tim, old pal! I see by your face that you have found the fearful stuff that Lura made her life, and that cost her life."

"Aye, Brack, that I did. 'Twas hidden well in a secret part of her desk, wrapped with wire it was, to look like a set of coils for some gadget to any spying penetray, that is why it was never noticed. 'Twill be hard to disguise as a seasoning for their mindless cooks; it has a bad smell."

"We have done harder tricks than that, Tim! Ben Uniaty has some contact with the Helpers; he will have a way and a mind to figure out that and more beside."

CHAPTER SIX
Reunited—And Work to Do

"THE mind," Bonur began, strutting a little and imitating wiser men he had heard give similar discourses, "is an electrical mechanism, as well as a record of past events; an electrical record."

Bill Flores looked askance at Bonur. It was incongruous to hear this gross creature break into an apparently technical discourse. But Bonur had had opportunities, and was not too stupid to take advantage of them. He had learned much from wiser men, men now dead, some at his hand. He had a superficial knowledge of the physics of the ancient mech in some part and what it was designed to do, as well as all the perverted uses to which it had been put since the long-ago when it was built.

Bill, after being admitted to the office of Benz the rodite, and soon thereafter arrested and thrown in prison, was now called before Bonur for questioning. Bill knew that Bonur was being very pleasant in hopes of allaying his suspicion and fear and making him talk freely. Bill realized that he had been arrested only because his name was his father's, and his father the brother of Pyotyr Flores. Then too, for all Bill knew, Bonur might have been the man who killed his father when he was a child. It had been someone in the palace, someone pumping his father as to the use of certain mech—and Bonur had acquired much of his education that way, from unwilling teachers. And his father had been an expert with and a collector of curious kinds of antique mech, and would have made a ripe victim for Bonur's school. Then, too, the watch ray had caught something of his, Bill's thoughts, and knew he was planning trouble. But after all, thinking about it and doing it were two different things.

Most of the people of Ontal wished Bonur and all his works to the devil for that matter.

Bonur continued with his discourse, the guards stood gravely at the door of the great room, the huge ro-mech at which Bonur was gesturing loomed before them in all its mystery of antique lost wisdom, its inhuman complexity; and Bill, like most others of the underworld who knew anything, knew that Bonur—no more than others—could build or even repair one bit of the ancient intricacy. Men like Brack and Tim were few and their secrets were guarded from generation to generation as well as they might where every thought may be read at any time over a ray. As for that, you can watch a plumber forever, but you will not learn to wipe a joint until you go to work for him. As Bonur went on with his discourse, strutting his superficial knowledge of the ancient science, a trim little slave girl tripped into the room and stood waiting nearby as if sent for.

Like most slaves of the caverns, she wore the ancient slave garb, a kind of Assyrian tunic, black, short and flare-skirted—an uncomfortable rig at best, but who worried about a slave's comfort? Some things never change in the caves.

"To one who has explored the inner workings of the mind with the visio-telaug—Bonur slurred the word as if not sure how to pronounce it—"the whole mental set-up called character can be reconstructed in any desired way by reimpressing all the records of the mind, all the fine films of sensitive flesh, with new and different summations from observed phenomena, can change the whole rule book by which the mind reasons out its action. I will demonstrate on little Sarah here; she has been disobedient, careless of my welfare. Come, Sarah."

RELUCTANTLY Sarah came forward, on her face a rebellious, independent and fearful expression. She dreaded what he was going to do to her.

"To show you what her character is now, a perhaps normal character but not one apt to be useful to me because she has decided I am not her friend. I will give her a few commands.

"Sarah, bite your arm till it bleeds!"

Sarah merely stared at him, did not obey.

"Sarah, strike the stranger between the eyes with your fist."

Sarah only kept staring wonderingly at Bonur, simply refusing such an incongruous order.

"You can see, Flores, that as a perfect tool, little Sarah leaves much to be desired. Help yourself to the sweets there on the table, Sarah."

Sarah got herself a handful of the bonbons, stood eating them.

"Now seat yourself at the instrument, my little sweetheart."

Bill's stomach turned, for he realized what was coming. He would have to watch it! But the girl obediently set herself in the great seat of strangely worked metal far too big for a human.

A ring of concentrically focused beams played on the girl's head where she sat, showing transparently blue and grey like pale flames, making of the yellow curls a weird nimbus about her head. On the twelve-foot screen at the side of the mech all the little thoughts of her brain showed separately as pictures, and one could hear, too, all the abstract roots of those complicated thought pictures working out into the complete thoughts that were the result of Sarah's rather simple but good mind at work.

Bonur directed an intense beam of blue absorptive ray upon her head, and made a swift adjustment of the dials below the screen. Instantly all the little patterns of intricately related thought-pictures changed, ran together, disappeared. Softly Sarah slumped, unconscious in the great seat.

Now, in place of the pictures and the thought heard before, began a new series of thoughts and memories from the record Bonur had started rotating in its spool within the mech. It was a record carefully prepared for this purpose, and all the obliterated scenes in her memory's screens were replaced now by its carefully prescribed memories. One could see the process horribly replacing the whole soul and self of the young girl; and read the purport of the thought as it was inscribed steadily on the mind that would no longer be her own, but a poor imitation of the real thing.

Nearly half an hour went by as the record repeated all its implied and intentional changes of logic; and the causes of future syllogism from past observed facts of nature were now all different. Bill knew her future acts would be based on an entirely new and simpler set of memories designed to produce the desired character—one wholly obedient to the whims of Bonur.

Sarah was at last released from the machine. She arose and stood before Bonur, a foolish, dog-like attitude of devotion and subjugation on her face.

"Bite yourself, Sarah!"

Sarah bent her fair head and sank her white teeth savagely in her own arm. The blood trickled down her wrist and dripped on the floor as she released the round young arm from her red-stained teeth.

"Strike Flores, here, between the eyes with your fist."

Bill got his hand in the way of the blow just in time.

"You see," Bonur turned to face Bill, "from now on she will do only as I command in a way she is sure will please me. I know because I myself am the author of every thought in her whole memory—all others have been destroyed, wiped out completely. All her action in the future will be a product of my own design, from a life-time of study of the mind."

BILL began to get the gist of the man's egoistic exhibition. He had never thought of the gross Bonur as a student, but it was evident that Bonur himself did think more highly of his mind than others gave him credit for. Bill sighed as he realized that this madman—a sadist, a moron, the leader of an evil cult that spread death and misery through the far-flung caverns—yet represented the highest, perhaps, development of science in the underworld. And the underworld has very different and greater opportunities by far than the surface world; insofar as the ancient mech is ready-made wisdom direct from the ancients who were far wiser than men. This was a rotten use to which his learning was put: to rob a girl of her young mind and replace it with the spirit of a yes-man, of a human robot.

Bonur was still talking, and though Bill was a little mystified yet as to why he had been called there since Bonur had not mentioned his recent half-formed plan—his immature impulse to find a way to rid Ontal of such things as Bonur—this mystery was fast clearing up. Bill listened to the rest of Bonur's bragging exposition in an agony of apprehension…did he intend to put him in the condition in which he had left Sarah or no?

"Her whole logic is a gift from my record, she has no other. The effect will wear off in time, but in a year or so I can play the record on her mind again and get the same result."

Bonur reached out and touched the girl's head with his fat black-bristled fingers, and her whole body wriggled ecstatically and shamelessly like a puppy's. She was obviously his completely devoted slave.

"Such a process is what I am going to do to you!" Bonur's smile was a sinister delight upon his face, his enjoyment the apex of the performance, what he had been working for. The sinking of the barb within the victim's flesh was the moment of joy for which he lived, to see the stricken look of the victim who knows there is no escape.

"When I get through, you are going to sign over your rights to Flore's holdings. Then you are going to go out and find the rest of your gang, and see what you can learn about such attempts to do away with me as you evolved in your mind. The mind that evolved that plan will cease to exist as such, and exist hereafter only as a dim memory of the far past, the extremely hazy past—a time when you did not know how to get along in the world. Getting along, now, will in your mind depend wholly on how well you serve my interests—and reward for your efforts will not enter your thoughts." Bonur's voice suddenly lost its silk and turned harsh, shrilly triumphant.

"Get into that seat, you young fool! You'll not be the man to murder Bonur. Sit down!"

Bill shuffled slowly forward. He could see no point in resisting, for several of Bonur's bullies lounged in the far doorway and he knew there was a roomful of armed men beyond for he had seen them on his way here. Besides, there were the slaves, standing about the room like near-nude statues, to put him into the mechanism's seat.

Bill put out his hand to reach the great arm of the ancient metal seat…when, as at a signal a strange, sudden *hum* came dramatically into the room from somewhere far outside!

Bonur leaped back, throwing up his hand, his mouth a round, startled "o" of ruby, revolting flesh. His whole face had swiftly become a mask of abject fear. The hum rose steadily to a deadly, insupportable whine—and Bill clapped his hands to his head, only to feel a mighty force tearing not only at his brain, but at every fiber of his body. The whole gloomy, rocky beauty of the ancient throne chamber of a forgotten God twisted into a deadly whirl and disappeared. He became a nothing, a flying nothing that did not think or know but felt terribly that it was no more existent.

BILL opened his eyes to see a stranger's bearded face bending solicitously over him.

"Where am I?"

"You are a long way from Bonur Golz. He may be ruler of this God-forsaken hole in the ground called Ontal, but he isn't ruler of this particular part of it. He has enough slaves and I can use a few well-meaning creatures like yourself. So I turned this ancient teleport mech on Bonur's private little hell, just as though I were an ancient scientist and knew what I was doing. But in truth I am just another man who usually wonders just what *will* happen when I push one of these time forgotten buttons."

"Teleportation?" Bill's voice was a bit awed. "I had heard that such mech existed, but since Bonur's ban on the use of any mech, we of the lower classes have not had much chance to know the nature of the ancient mech."

"You're not lower class!" The bearded man was smiling at Bill hospitably, but his mind was obviously somewhere else.

"I have become so, since my father's death and now my uncle's at Bonur's hands. My father had quite a store of the rare kinds of mech. He collected peculiar and little known types of machinery from all the far caves and was expert at its use. But Bonur, I guess, wanted his wonder mech, and did not want my father alive. Anyway he died or disappeared some years ago, and we could never find a trace of him. So we laid it at Bonur's door and went on living. Now he has killed my uncle."

"I know your history, son. Yes, it was Bonur killed your father, after long weeks of torment in his telaugs to get the last iota of information on what he knew of his machines. But let me introduce my fellow conspirators. First we must conceal the teleport, just in case."

The old man pulled a lever in the wall. The tall metal enigma of intricate, impossible construction sank slowly into the floor. About it as it sank Bill could see the shimmer of mercury, which finally covered it entirely.

"Why the mercury?" asked Bill.

"Same diffraction as the metal of the teleport to penetrays. These walls are of the impenetrable metal of the ancient's ray armor, but there do exist some samples of the rare ray-mech designed to penetrate just this metal. Bonur has one of these rare mech. He keeps it in his vaults, which protects us, as he gives a look only occasionally and finds nothing wrong, for we are forewarned by men who watch him and others with similar rare rays. Bonur is going now to get his private ray out and start his own private search for us. He will not find anything because that type of ray will not convey thought through this metal, and the rays that will penetrate visually do so imperfectly and hence things hidden as this mech is in mercury seem but solid blocks of opacity—or of glass—all a shimmer with unseeableness. That is why the mercury. It conceals nearly anything sunk in it from such rays because of its particular kinship to the metal of the teleport mech. We use it thus to hide many things. We have our ways, which you will learn before you become of use to us."

Through the door came a familiar long-nosed slim man, smiling with his rotten teeth.

"This fellow," the bearded man continued, "is Brack Longen. Ah, you have met before! I am surprised. I must be getting very forgetful. And this woman is called Nita—and a very beautiful girl she is too—who sat and starved because she thought you were dead! Ah, I see you have met before! And I had meant to introduce Tim Shanter here, but I see you are too busy kissing Nita to pay any attention to the red-haired grease monkey anyway. You have probably met him too, I suppose."

Old Ben Uniaty was laughing as he withdrew from the chamber of the teleport and beckoned to Brack and Tim to leave the reunited lovers alone.

"OH, BILL, it has been years, it seemed! But only a short week or two, I guess, really."

"It has been years for me, Nita, and I have lost track of time, too. I know I have acquired a head of grey hair, by the feel of it."

"I have too, you big lug!" Her arms went around him and that glorious feeling that is always present when two meet after long absence swallowed their separate selves in oneness.

Outside, the bearded one and Brack were talking.

"I can't understand teleportation. It seems to me matter must be destroyed to become a part of a ray that penetrates even rock."

"It is a miraculous mechanism that I don't fully understand myself. But you must have noticed in using penetrays at one time or another that they have a faculty of picking up odors—turpentine, chlorine, or worse—and carrying the odor along with them even through miles of rock?"

"Yes, I swung a penetray into a skunk one night when I was surreptitiously helping the surface men search for a lost child in a wood over-head. I was stank out properly."

"Stunk," corrected Tim, listening.

"Well, it smelled so bad I couldn't return to the search for nearly an hour. Stank or stunk, a penetray will carry an odor."

"Well, the ancients must have observed this phenomena early in their work with penetrative rays and developed its potential use as the years went by. From it they finally developed a way of sending things over long distances by ray. They seem to have a ray that dissolves matter. The penetrays carry the components back over the return path—you know how the double rays work as a full circuit. The scanner, tuned to the subject, in this case Bill, reassembles the matter in its original pattern in the chamber of the mech. The whole thing happens so swiftly that death does not result if the object is carefully brought into tight focus. You remember the care with which I adjusted the focus upon the chair while the girl was in it? It was temptation not to steal Bonur's favorite slave girl. But I cannot pull the stunt too often, and was afraid Bonur would do Bill in before I got a chance to get him too. It is the telesolidograph screen which makes the whole possible and you are as familiar with that screen as I am."

"It would certainly be nice if we had one of the ancient race's techs for a few days, eh? Long enough to clean up this sink called Ontal."

"Maybe we can do the job ourselves, Brack. Your latest plan looks good to me."

"Look, instead of slipping that poison to the cooks, which I believe to be a plan wrought with problems at best, why not impregnate the meat with the poison through the use of the teleport?"

"Brack, I am afraid of the odor. That stuff has a mean smell—and besides the teleport is selective; it won't send everything. If there were minerals of certain kinds, the obscuring odorous material we use to cover up the poison might also be left out as well as some necessary part of the poison composition. The substance might thus be changed. The mech is peculiarly designed for certain purposes and for no others. It is adjusted carefully by the ancients for inclusion of everything necessary to life, it leaves out nearly all else. For instance, such a teleportation was used by the ancients for a health treatment because it leaves out toxic materials of certain kinds. They had the mech so adjusted by field attunement inside. For instance it makes a young man younger, and an old man young again because the body that has passed through its magnetic torsion and rearranging does not any longer contain the age-causing radioactives which it had at the sending end. You know my age, Brack?"

"Why, I had thought 45 or so. Tell me truthfully, how old are you?"

"I was 85 yesterday. Due solely to yearly teleportation's of just a few feet distance with the mech. That is one reason I keep it concealed in its bath of mercury."

"God, it is the long sought secret of the ancient's immortality!"

"It is one of them, Brack. That is why I do not want these evil overlords of ours to get it. Even death would not rid us of them, then. They would live on and on—always evil! It would mean the end of all future hope for men if evil got immortality before good!"*

"BEN, I have done much reading in my lifetime and I have read in old stories of medieval times how the elves and the goblins—the antics of cavern people imitating such things, I mean—played with the people above ground by teleporting them and levitating them. The ancient custom of Walpurgis when we and the surface followers all worshipped together in some secluded spot, and the custom included transportation for the surface people to the place by either teleportation or levitation depending on whether the invited one was outside or

---

*Just another reason why modern techs must get down into the caves and clean it out—the modern evil down there is hot on the trail of just that secret, which would mean the end of hope for the future of men, in truth. At present the worst are said to use baby blood transfusions to fight age.—Author.

or indoors. When the invited one remained indoors, teleportation was used, as taking them through doors and windows by levitation was apt to be seen and commented on to their detriment, as well as the fact the closed windows and doors were often in the way."

"Yes, once much more of this mech was in common use, down here. But misuse and destruction has made many kinds of mech rare. It is too sad that we have not the surface world's organizations of benevolent nature to organize and study and understand and the science that lies in such machines, and save it for the future as well as make us all wiser and healthier and infinitely longer-lived by its use."

"But speaking of the poison, you think to place it in the meat by teleport just wouldn't work?"

"No, it just wouldn't."

"Well, we can get it to the cooks anyway. And then goodbye to the whole mess in the Stem palace!"

"And once more the Stem will be open to travel to the surface by anyone with business on the surface."

"But, if we open the Stem to the knowledge of the surface, the reactionaries in other cavern cities who now keep the ancient secret would attack us?"

"I think not. Soon similar plans will be afoot in every important settlement over the whole continent. Something different for all of us will come of it."

"One would think so. It must be all very carefully arranged, and the coup only known of by men like ourselves. You are to tell only those whose lives are already forfeit to the rulers if captured—those whose nature is, like ours, wholly oppositional to the nature of the evil bosses."

"Explain the teleport some more—I would understand it. I might have to fix one for my use some day."

"Well, they developed this carrying of atoms through rocks and of her solids until they could blast a solid with ray of such great pressure that the solid melted, flowed between the force lines of the rays—was carried along the path of the ray to its destination. There, when the pressure of the ray was removed by a counter force-flow, the substance was deposited as matter again."*

BILL and Nita came through the doorway beneath the great carven mermaids into the metal chamber where the bearded man waited between Brack and Tim. Bill bowed low before him in a manner little seen these days, but once much used among the elder folk of the cavern world when evil was less the way of life, and benevolence and wisdom more.

"Your name, I take it, is Ben Uniaty. I was told by friends long ago: when in trouble go about with the thought, 'I want Ben Uniaty' and you will soon find a way to help me unseen. I had forgotten, or else you had heard from me long ago."

----

*Rocks can be sent through rocks, which seems impossible, because of the nature of telesolidograph focus which brings the pressure to bear only at the focus of all the rays. They are no longer rocks under ray pressure; their parts elongate, stretch, become like photons or sub-photons, are carried along as part of the ray flow. So it is that matter may be sent along a ray to be precipitated once again—the scanning apparatus directs a small flow of this dissolving ray over the focus of the teleport solidograph receiver, unseen at the subject's end of the ray but visible in the screen as a solid. Apparently the whole thing happens within the screen, but in reality tremendous forces are under remote control at the other end of the ray and as the scanner dissolves the solidograph image in the screen, the matter disappears at the other end. If the thing happened lowly, living matter could not survive the long time-interval—it would bleed as the ray tore it away bit by bit and reassembled it at the other end.

The heart of the thing is a scanner of intricate and rapid nature, coupled with the telesolidograph, which makes an image of anything upon which it is focused, anywhere in three dimensions. The, scanner controls the dissolving ray at that end, and likewise controls a duplicate scanner which contains a precipitating ray which neutralizes the pressure of the ray bearing the matter, and thus causes a precipitation which is controlled entirely by the speed and quantity of the pickup scanner at the other end—though both scanners are located right in the machine. That is as near as I can come to describing the apparatus to you.—Author.

"We did not know the straits you and Nita were in. You said nothing, you appeared now and then, we thought nothing of you. When we learned, it was too late."

"I want earn my way here, to pull my weight. You fellows are taking tremendous risks in what you do, and I think I have an idea where your work tends. I want to be part of it."

"We both do," said Nita.

"You both will," said Ben Uniaty. "I do not risk or use my treasured immortality for nothing. You must be of value to me to repay me, for the risk I take is much greater than a mortal one. Remind me, Nita, to send you through the teleport for a short distance so that you do not age at a greater rate than Bill. So long as you are my people, you will be sent through the mech at regular intervals to preserve your youth. The transportation leaves behind the cause of age.

"You may not go out of these metal walls even for an instant. Everyone in here has either been brought by the teleport or has very carefully guarded his thought on the way here. Since we are embarking on this enterprise, we plan on sealing up all the doors entirely with impervious metal, and going in and out entirely by the teleport. That is the only way to be sure we are safe here. But we may decide to leave the city entirely. It depends on the way things go. Meanwhile, no trips out to rummage about through the deserted levels as all of us love—to search for the time-forgotten wonders of our elder race. No, you *must* not—it is a firm order!"

"We will not," said Nita sweetly, and Bill nodded affirmation.

"Now to work, both of you. First, for Bill there is an assembly to which some odd parts are missing. Brack will go and search for the rest of the mech when he knows what to look for. As your father's son you are a valuable man, Bill. You can tell Brack what to get to furnish me with many new mech.

"For Nita, there is cooking, and when we relax there is dancing for us to do. I surmise Nita will soon become the most valuable thing in our lives. We are well supplied; I steal stocks of food from the stores of the brigand rulers of the city—and they never miss them. The slaves are afraid to report anything missing for fear they will be blamed.

"Brack, you have your errand. The day of the feast draws near, time is short. Get it done, and I will stand guard with the watch-ray so that nothing happens. The hour is almost at hand but two more—and you must be there or I cannot help get the thing done. On your way!"

Once again the great teleport mech rose from its bed of quicksilver and Brack stepped into the sending chamber within the metal of the mech. Ben Uniaty pressed a stud, and Brack disappeared as if by magic. It *was* magic, the same ancient magic that has been worked by hidden men like Old Ben Uniaty, and by others like Bonur Golz, since the first Egyptian pressed the first bricks out of wet clay and straw. For it was such a one as him who gave the Pharaoh frogs and blood and death for his first born to release his people, the Jews, so long ago.

The tradition is an old one and the mech to do such miracles has suffered much, but the caverns are vaster in extent than the surface world by far, and no man knows what may be found by search in the endless warrens of darkness. So always, though the mech is destroyed by fearful men to prevent anyone using it to kill them, there is more of the wonder machines to be found and used against such a Pharaoh, or against a modern Bonur.

AT THE same time that Brack was setting out on his journey, Bonur Golz sat peering up into the dark water of Long Island Sound with a long-range penetray. Up there in the dark water a spaceship had landed—unseen, drifting down like a falling leaf. Inside some strange, kind people were listening with their instruments to the radio reports of the war and the peace conference. An officer said to another—"Fighting lubbers!"*

---

* By lubbers is meant men not knowing space travel-space lubbers. They speak English (there are many traveling space who do speak English) having left earth centuries ago on space ships from the cavern's stores and never returned to earth. The strange visitors were English-speaking wanderers of space, accidentally coming back to the place their forefathers left.—Author.

"Fighting lubbers, these earthmen! Makes one want to give them a hand. They seem to mean well about their world peace."

Beside him his wife spoke. "Let me read one of their minds—one who has never known that anyone could peer inside and read his thought. Oh—he senses me, he blushes and looks around. It is a darling mind—it is perfectly open. What an innocent such a mind is. It never has concealed a thought!"

Even as they talked, Bonur reached up with the great space-ray weapon inside the Stem palace and wiped out all the life in the ship. Bonur had no wish for these visitors to contact surface men—for their weapons in the hands of surface men meant trouble and taxes and interference and war to Bonur. It was custom so to destroy all who might bring the two worlds together.

That same hour that Bonur murdered the big ship-load of strangers in the Sound, and left the space ship lie there in the dark, deep water never to be known by any but himself, a rich young she-devil of his acquaintance was putting out the life and flame of liberty burning in the breast of a young man of Ontal. Very slowly she burned his life away, asking always, "Are you loyal?" and answered always, "Only to the sane!"

She knew what he meant, for none of Ontal ever pretended that the bunch of madmen who had seized control of the Stem under Bonur were sane. For Bonur was the best and sanest of them all, and even so was a mad beast. They were very stupid, very cruel, and very active in their oppression, killing all who showed the slightest disposition to resent their innumerable and constant injuries.

Just before she finished him off by playing live steam over his dying body, he shrieked, "And I had hoped!"

He meant that it was futile to hope for anything but misery and death in the underworld, and he was right regarding those parts of it with which he was familiar of late years. He meant that he felt those idealists who try to keep the flame of revolt for liberty alive—the flame of effort toward a better life for the miserable lesser members—were false dreamers who had misled him. But he was wrong, for we must try.

Not far above the dying man, on the surface, another young man lay sleeping. From Max, where his rollat was parked just outside the City of Ontal beside the Stem-way, a ray reached up and touched the young man's head. From another direction Max sent a ray toward the woman who was torturing the "traitor" to death, and transferred the sensations of torment into sleeping thoughts of the young man of surface New York.

The dream died out and left him gasping, flat in the bed and wondering where he had been to get such a case of sunburn. He was burned, he thought—and he felt himself all over—every inch of his skin should have been fiery red and sore as a boil. His relief at finding his pain had been a dream was short lived. For even as his exploring, fearful hands felt of his body, the heat began to increase, and he was not dreaming. Dreams are darn funny things when they keep on after you wake up! He tried to get up, but the heat was increasing—and he could not rise! In a few minutes he died, his whole body a smoldering char. His night-dress was not even scorched when the coroner examined the charred corpse.*

DEEP under the house where the man died of a dream, Max, the mad little ghoul who represented quite a large part of the evil life of the caves, Max, the sub-human with a fat belly and round pursed mouth and fat hips and womanish look, laughed and laughed at the mystification on the faces of the people as to how a man burned to death in his own bed without even scorching the bed or his own night clothes. And the very insane little ghoul left the old induction-ray mech with the "burning" button he had found still running its ray up into the rock above, though he had shifted it to a lower level so that they should not learn about it above. Then he went off to search beside the old

----

* See the notes of Charles Fort for several of these deaths.—Author.

beside the old aqueduct for a big white lizard to stay his hunger till he had a chance to bargain with the trader in Ontal for food for his gems.

Also searching the watercourse that brought Ontal's water into her fountains and into the basins that flowed in the houses were some of the starving of Ontal who had no love for such as Max. And it was not long before Max was roasting over a spit—for desperation has few squeams. Max had known better than to leave the screen of his weapon ray—but he had been hungry.

Tonight was the feast of the Satanists, in the palace of the Stem. Max would not be there. Several other visiting evil ones found their way into the cook-pots of Ontal men. And the fact that Bonur guaranteed them safe conduct was enough to cause their death; and hunger is hunger.

But the Cultists came as ever. The city was filling up with them, and the police were busy protecting them—very busy! For if they were understood anywhere, it was in Ontal, where they gathered for their annual Sabbath.

Over all Ontal hung a blanket of evil thought from their interlocking telaug beams, as they watched everywhere for the attacks that among them were nearly continuous, for men like them are always on the watch. And their thought was utterly not good, as it watched and argued and gloated over Ontal.

Those same days before the feast a rheumatic fever that had been festering and killing in a town in Carolina moved northward, a victim here, a fatality there, and an old doctor watched its progress and wondered why it had ceased attacking people in his town and moved so rapidly northward. But that it had some human agency behind it was of course too ridiculous an idea to talk of to anyone.

But I wish the good doctor could have seen the mad little wight who rolled slowly along in a rollat the size of a circus van; and seen the collection of weird apparatus he had gathered in his wanderings through the endless wonder-world of the caverns. Then he might have believed that a disease can be simulated by a combination of rays. Yes, it might have occurred to him—but that there was a reason for the terrible series of painful deaths from rheumatic fever he would not have learned, for the mad little man driving the rollat had no reason in his own mind. Reason had been bred out of his makeup by a long line of mad, wild wanderers of the caverns. But the lust to kill and torment—that had *not* been bred out, nor had its terrible consequences ever reached his mind. For were not the surface men helpless against him. Yes, they were.

It was this same madman who crashed the plane bearing Carole Lombard and some twenty army officers into the side of a mountain near the California line. That was an enjoyable incident for him, and no one even chased him for it, for he does not exist to the minds of surface men. It required but the easiest sort of "tamper" work with the delicate instruments of the panel in front of the pilot. And his rays that could read the pilot's mind could also direct the needles of his instruments into those patterns most terrifying to the pilot. Terrifying because true when properly manipulated. Ah man, how superior are those of the caverns to us of the surface. Can they not kill us at will?

CHAPTER SEVEN
Feast of the Satanists

NOT far from the Palace of the Stem was a place that sold beer and wines to the staff of the great house. It stood now nearly empty for it was an hour when most were busy preparing for the great feast of the evil cult that Bonur used as his vehicle to power, his avenues of wide information from the whole cavern world, as well as searchers of the far, deserted and unknown caverns for powerful mech as yet not in his collection.

Inside sat Brack, tonight wearing his thought-hiding device. It was humming inside his head a song that he liked, and he listened to the soft words, taken from an old record that had lain in the metal room when he had moved in. In his pocket were several little shakers, little containers like salt holders with swivel tops, and in his mind was a hidden purpose—those tops must bare their holes over food for all the evil in Ontal.

Into the room came one of the staff, an under-cook, one of the men for whom he waited. These lowlier of the palace staff were men who been operated upon in the mind, to make them less apt to hate their overlords and hence less apt to be tools for just such a scheme as Brack was hatching. The result of the operation in this case was a man who could not remember what happened yesterday, but who could carry out orders without trouble until tomorrow, when all was forgotten. He was not the best of servants, but his short memory was a useful feature since he forgot any hate for any injury done him. Called ro, there are many such, but they are not the same creature that was meant by the ancient word; they are a modern development of the life in the Masked World. Once a man has been cut as was this one, he has little sense or reason, but he does retain such ingrained thought habits as his trade—in this case, cooking.

The cutting of the brain centers to produce such characters is itself a kind of trade, and there are many "cuts" producing different types of "ro." Those centers of the brain most apt to cause trouble by independent thinking against their unwelcome masters are "cut" by a penetrative ray that acts somewhat like a surgeon's electric needle. Connecting nerves in the brain are cut. So the man who entered was a thing that was not strictly human. Bonur's device was a variant of a superior method of producing the same result, a man in appearance, but a man who has lost his birthright of reason from a willful brain mutilation by his master. He can talk almost naturally, but cannot remember or reason except in the most simple animal-like way. He can ask for beer or tobacco. The constant repetition of such incidents in his daily life has impressed them on his feeble faculties.

As soon as he entered Brack spoke to him, smiling, for such creatures have no suspicions or imagination and accept all things at their surface value.

"Ho, cook, come and drink with me. It is a lonesome business, this sitting down to be merry and finding no one to chaff with."

"Yes, sir," answered the cook, beaming great pleasure to be noticed as a human being, for the "ro" are rather despised members of society, a thing lower than a natural, unmutilated slave.

The cook sat his fat body down on the bench beside Brack and smiled, but nothing in his poor mutilated head functioned to make talk, and smiling was as far as he ever got with conversation.

TONIGHT Brack had disguised not only his thoughts so that his mind thought steadily through the tiny record of the mind of a young roustabout rummy of the taverns taken by Brack some weeks before, but his face was carefully disguised to look like another person entirely.

The bitter lines of his mouth and face were smoothed out with a face-wax too thin to be seen, his gray hair was dyed a good black, and his clothing was a flashy young fop's, which did not look out of place on his lean and graceful figure. His long nose was changed with a carefully built up bridge and hook. His thoughts were as idle a bunch of nonsense as ever occupied a man with nothing to do but enjoy an evening from his work—songs and idle nothings. The watch ray took one cursory glance at him and dismissed him from their minds.

The cook listened raptly to everything Brack said, and as promptly forgot it. Brack entertained him with a long and fulsome discourse on cookery the world over; he had spent several hours reading a cook book called the "World Traveler's Cook Book" to prepare himself for this deed.

Then Brack went into an even lengthier discourse on "seasoning as an art" and wound up with saying that in all his travels he had found but one great perfect flavoring to bring out all the savor of meat—and he had a goodly lot of it in his pocket.

The cook reached out a great red hand and took a pinch from the open shaker in Brack's hand. He smelled it, rubbed it between his fingers, looked at it long, close to his eyes—then held it there before him as he explained that never in all his wide experience with cooking and condiments had he seen anything like it or knew what it might be. Brack was well aware of this, for the cook's mind was far from encyclopedic and every flavor in the encyclopedia was incorporated in the stuff to hide the nauseous odor of the poison.

Brack held his tongue with an effort as the cook popped the stuff into his mouth to get the flavor—and signed his death warrant thereby. But Brack's conscience soothed itself with the hidden thought that many better by far would die did Bonur live on, and Brack let be.

Brack gave him the shakerful of death's powder amid profuse thanks from the humble fellow, then furnished him with a couple of "spares" in case he desired to use it at the feast, so that there would be "plenty to go around" and went on his way swiftly, not wishing to linger there after the deed was done. The only thing left was to remind the nearly mindless fellow over the telaug beam to place it on the meat this night of Satan's raising, this night when the devil himself came to visit his followers.

THE hour of the feast has arrived, and about the great, gloomy rock chamber hang the decorations for the bloody revels to be held.

The ancient carvings on the walls, polished by the later hands of the good men of Ontal, are smoke-darkened now from the many fires of the recurrent Demon feasts—and every feast an orgy of blood letting for their inverted pleasure senses.

Tonight was to be a greater indulgence in the art of torment for pleasure than any other previous.

In the center of the tremendous, profusely and rather horribly decorated chamber was the great red metal statue of Satan which would tonight be reanimated with the actual force called Satan, and worshipped by the cult.

The decorations, among other horrifics, included stuffed human figures—horrible and poorly executed samples of the underworld taxidermy applied to the human.

Slave girls hastened about their task of strewing straw about the floor, of setting all the places with many odd dishes peculiar to the feast, the blood goblets, the finger bowls filled with scented water, the sauces and condiments. The sulphuric perfumes alleged to be present at such events were not present, but instead some very stimulating perfumes were brought for the occasion from the rare stores of unguents and scents of the ancients themselves. Some of these were famous for producing in weak modern men reactions sometimes called panurgic.

The living decorations were all nicely writhing and the stim current flowing into them through the wires of the niches where they hung, so that they were like statues brought to a strange and terrible activity by some fearful magic—by the terrific stimulation of the ancient life-energy force-flows.

The red lilies of this feast strewed the floor and stood in great vases whereever a place might be found for them, and about the statue of Satan himself rested a great bank of the black lilies of death so dear to his own black heart.

The cook with whom Brack had had such an important conversation hastened in from his fires in the kitchens and looked over all the preparations to make sure that everything was going all right and smiled and bowed as the red priest himself sauntered slowly through, strewing some blood from a thing called an aspergillis over the floor as he walked. I surmise the blood was thoroughly accursed by some ritual that was pure flummery of course, but what he was saying in the ancient tongue called Demonlang would curl the whiskers of the great opponent, Yahveh himself.

Bonur himself waddled through the hall, and stopped to talk to the red masked priest—who was also Nake, his right hand, under the horned mask.

"Has all the flummery been well attended to, Nake, you faker?"

"Quite, quite, chosen of Satan, quite."

"It will come off all right, eh? I don't want to miss the sacrifices."

"I rather enjoy them myself, my lord, though it seems a great waste of good flesh. But as you say, we get the value out of the dupes for the trifling price of a few slaves' lives. Odd, eh, how the old ways and customs persist. In spite of Time's dull sweep, custom persists. We could not hold the wild ones of the far caverns without this foolishness, and they would not bring us gold or slaves, or the rare mech and the ancient jewels did we not put on a good show for them."

"God knows what they will bring in next. Last week from a cavern under Mexico an ignorant, unwashed idiot of the maddest stripe brought in a solid gold robot as a gift to the Red One. For Satan himself—all that value—and without the slightest idea of asking anything in return but Satan's good wishes."

"CURIOUS things, some of those robots the old ones manufactured. One cannot imagine what their uses might have been."

"This one was a curious sample of their workmanship. Heavy—and the mech inside made it walk and talk as lightly and as beautifully as a young girl. It is a beautiful thing; that is, it was. I activated the mechanism inside and it walked up to me, peered into my eyes in the most human way, and began to talk in the ancient tongue; you know, you have heard some of the mech talk as if they were imbued with actual life. I know little of the tongue, but I know enough to know that this robot was a kind of prophet, and that it foretold some doom, some kind of curse. It worried me for a time… And as the robot went on and on, the ominous tone of the voice, the terrible, fear-creating gestures of the thing, the seemingly actual life in the robot struck me with fear and with an anger as at a human being! I ordered the thing cast into the melting pots and made into bullion. Later I was sorry, but you know how fearful some of that mech can be when it runs amuck. Well, I think we are better off without that robot around. Maybe it was just a machine, but sometimes one believes in magic when one sees the wonders those ancients created."

Nake mused aloud, "She spoke in the ancient tongue, and seemed to prophesy doom, eh? That worry's me, Bonur."

"Ah, it's silly. She was probably created to act a part in a play or something; one can't believe a mental thing that has lain around for untold centuries in the dark of a deserted cave could think, could prophesy—it's a ridiculous idea... Just the same, Nake, keep your eyes open."

"It might be well to keep our eyes open without any robot gloom to make us, Master."

"You're right, Nake. Plenty of people would be happy to see us dead."

"Those ancients were wondrous wise, Bonur."

"Don't try to worry me, Nake! And don't get the idea you should inherit my power if something happened. I keep my ears open, Nake."

"Have your joke, Master. But just the same, be careful, we would all be lost without you; all the strings of our lives are in your hands. If you should stumble, we would all fall."

"And don't forget that, Nake!" Bonur walked off chuckling, but Nake did not take the strange account so lightly, for Nake knew a thing or two, himself. Such unbelievable things had sometimes been accomplished by the antique work that one could believe anything of it. Nake had once seen a machine that turned out (from a mass of vegetable and animal matter thrown into the hopper) a living thing that was manlike. An intelligent, human-looking product had arisen living from the machine.

Nake had known enough of the ancients' mental slant to have the thing killed, for what a thinking product of their handiwork would do to evil was not unknown to Nake. Too, there was an old tale that the ancients had had the power of foretelling the future. Well, Nake decided, he would hope they did *not* do it with a machine that was built like a golden girl.

AN HOUR later the feast was in full swing, the woman who served as the Altar of the Red One, was well nigh worn out with the countless dishes that had rested on her for the look and nod of the robot who was supposed to be the great Satan himself animating the metal statue.

Flames roared from a full hundred cooking fires about the walls, and over each revolved a spit, and on the spits were pieces of flesh. The cruel customs of the age-old worship of the deification of evil required the eating of human flesh, and the nature of the caverns intermittent and often nonexistent food supplies had done much to perpetuate the custom.

The woman who has served as the altar before the terrible figure of the Devil rises and begins "The Dance of the Demoness." That dance of a soul becoming the Devil's ecstatic property—that dance, for sheer wanton lust of the flesh, for sheer all-out casting off of all spiritual and moral restraint (such as lingers in all surface men's equivalent performances in some fashion) can give the mind a view into the true fiery lure of Hell. The dance of the blood-dabbled priestess of the Sabbath is the beginning of an orgy such as few men of normal mind ever see—and stay sane.

Remember that neither the dancer nor the devotees of the cult of blood and torture and death are in any way the products of an environment akin to our own.

Both the dancer and the glittering-eyed maniacs who watch her portray the casting aside of all human feeling and the donning of the full character of the "demoness" are people raised in an ancient tradition of the worship of evil as a way of life, a belief and worship more intensely indulged mentally than any Christian or other surface worship. Their minds—since little children under the absolute control of ray-workers themselves more debauched than one can imagine—have been shaped in a mold of inhuman thought forms by the powerful control beams of the telaug till reactions inconceivable to us have replaced every natural reaction within their minds. Only when seen on the thought screens of the ancient telemach can it be believed.

There is much of this dance and of the orgy that follows that cannot be described here for obvious reasons—such as the prostration of the priestess before, and union with the metal, horrible, human inhumanity of the form of the Great Demon Lord.

I believe that evil should be brought out into the light and looked at—but there are those who, perhaps for reasons of fear, or reasons you may imagine for yourself, would object. One often thinks they must be in league with the devil themselves to throw such a shadow of obstruction before attempts to portray the true picture of evil life as it actually is.

However, picture for yourself the priestess-dancer presenting the sacrificial babe, squawling and kicking, to the great ugly robot that is supposed to be the vehicle in which the Devil returns to life for an evening. Picture the madness of the foul murder that follows.

Picture the audience, sprawling in a great crowd, their eyes drinking in the utterly savage scene. Remember that this scene has taken place exactly the same since before we had a Santa Claus. Before the Egyptians had a Pharaoh, this same devil worship in the caves was old.

Remember they are the children of a race which has for ages had beneficial rays of great curative powers in their ignorant hands, and never found a way of getting one bit of the medically beneficial ray-generator mech to surface men; to men who might study, copy and manufacture it; develop from the science of the past a science that would set man back upon the path to racial greatness—but, instead, this hidden race has be-deviled and obstructed men always out of fear of what men might do to them for their deeds if ever they got power. They think of themselves as "demons" and of us as "men!"

Always they have feared to even tell their surface brothers of the wonders of the ancient science. A foolish, dog-in-the-manger attitude has kept the ancient wisdom secret and excluded from wide study all these endless, wasted centuries.

Nor shall I describe the "beauty" of this dancing "demoness." It may be just as well you cannot see her as she is (as I might describe her were the censors willing) but I do not believe that.

REMEMBER always that such as she and many like her still *live,* and still have power over men like yourself—the power of life and death. They *really* exist, and practice their ancient evil seduction in many, many places under our earth. Picture yourself falling into her hands—would she have some use for you? Not at all—only as a thing from which pain could be wrung.

Then realize that still today stupid men of the surface serve such beings in ways you may guess at—and serve them to our detriment.

Picture the burning wretches over the coals whipped even as their flesh crisps in the searing heat. Realize that they are only the preliminary scenes that lead up to the main events. Picture the beautiful maidens (sometimes stolen from the surface) who wrestle with ravening tigers and other beasts and die bloodily just as they did in ancient Rome, before a more bloodthirsty, more stupid and savage group of madmen and madder women than ever graced Rome's perfumed arenas.

Then realize that these same spectators are people who whisper and lie nightly to our own state officers, our elected rulers, and get them to *really believe* that a secret science—from the "stars" of "space," mind you—has come to earth and is working with people to make something out of them. Or that they are selected "Fausts" and must do evil or die!

Realize that earth has more horrible perils still to struggle against than ever the Germans were and we will win. For we are neither few nor weak, and we, the white magic, have all that power and ancient heritage, too. And it shall be ours for real study on the surface if ever the evil of the caves can be defeated and the entrances freed of such as the Bonur pictured here.

Some of these dying slave girls were not so long ago decoratively wobbling across Fifth Avenue on their high heels. Now, they are on police blotters as "Missing, left note saying—Going to end it all, disappointed in love." Any obvious fabrication will do to evade the necessity of admitting publicly that the "Marvs"* got another one. Men who are men enough to admit there is an underworld are what we need. They have heard of it endlessly, it is well known among many classes of society and quite openly talked about. But for our learned professors and wise medical men and ever-right historians to admit that something they hadn't been taught in school could yet be true is too much to expect.

Police know it, I am sure, but can't say it, can't locate the trouble when they know it exits, and have given up all mention of it as a hopeless job. Well it isn't hopeless, but it was to medieval men. They had no science to understand the wonder world. We must dare to face what we know to be true.

Picture then that these dying girls are still but preliminary scenes to the "real stuff" of the evening. What do you think the real treat of the evening will be? I can't tell you—not the most terrible, but I will try to describe one of the lesser of these sadistic treats if I can get away with it.

Picture a square formed of oaken four-by-fours, held upright and of a size to enclose a human figure at the shoulders. A strong young man is lashed firmly to the oaken cross pieces—spread-eagled—with many stout ropes binding him. He is lashed firmly, arms and legs tightly held within the frame. Now picture a super-stimulator ray played upon his muscles of such strength that he leaps and leaps again in gradually increasing strength against the stout frame till the oak *splinters,* his arms and legs break, the blood spouts from arteries torn asunder by spasms of a fearful and mighty force which no human body can live through.

----

*"Marvs" is slum slang for the well-known "voices."—Author.

Picture the hereditarily mad group of people who have enjoyed just such scenes over and over back and back into time—before the very stones of the pyramids were quarried from their beds. That is the savage life which still persists in all its ancient evil in some parts of the caverns under our feet.

Picture that this scene of death is not yet the climax of the Satanists' feast. What then do you think the climax will be?

Such are the devil ray of the caverns, though their way of life has made them few, still they are the mightiest threat to civilization that lives "on" or "in" this planet. They control vast areas of our surface governments, and surface men can not touch them with any weapon they know—indeed when they know of them, fear even to speak of them. Police and others who should will not admit of their existence. If they want to be secret no lowly policeman or news editor cares to say them nay.

Truth is, there is no more stupid or evil people on earth than the evil ray people, and only the good sane groups of ray defending us with the mighty mechanisms of the chasms below us save us from a life of degradation unimaginable except to those who have seen what sadist ray-men can do to make life unnecessary to the normal human in their power. Thank God there are some good ray people.

CHAPTER EIGHT
Feast of Poison!

THE black smoke rises from torches set about the great hall, in slow evil twists, and the yellow light is shed fitfully over feasters, who are mostly rather small men, often deformed and horrible to the eye, for the strange heredity of the caverns has brought fearful changes to the forms of many great lumpish skins, twisted limbs, and beast-like faces. They do not often let surface men see these deformities, even when they are people of good will. But this "bunch," clad in rags and dirt, diseased, with madness glaring from their eyes, is the worst of the People of the abyss—the Satanists.

They are the lowest things that earth has bred in the shape of man. They do not have the sense to keep clean, or to think as men do in any way. Their value lies in a cleverness and quickness, a knowledge of the uses of the ancient mech they have grown up with, and a willingness to use the same in any vile way the master bids. This cleverness and quickness of the hands and eyes is something they acquire very young or die. For the mad ones of the wild stretches of the caves—and most of them are wild, unexplored—survival depends upon constant watchfulness and skill with a ray beam similar in some ways to the art of fencing with a rapier. No training can make up for the skill acquired by the mad ones in their constant fighting with the mech-ray from their childhood on.

To a surface man, the fat, waddling figure of Bonur, the Boss of Ontal, just one of the great cities of the underworld, would have looked comic. But he was fearful and deadly of appearance to those who knew him.

Bonur was heavy with fat, and his hips were much wider than his shoulders. About his waist was a very wide jeweled belt, and in the belt was thrust a multitude of peculiar weapons. As he walked, the weapons—built for men of a size three times Bonur's short six feet—swung and banged about his knees.* His robe, of a scintillating, florid fabric from the east, embroidered over with great passion flowers; his fat pouter chest hung with a glitter of ornaments; his broad red face, dark with the slovenly stubble of his beard; his drooping jowls hanging over his jeweled collar: his whole appearance was ludicrous comic opera to a surface man's eye. But it was not comic opera to the men of the underworld. They had to face this man as their ruler, the lord of life and death whose whim was law. All the ignorant bestiality of his nature was their problem, to placate, to please, to get along with somehow.

---

*The elder race seems to have averaged about twenty feet, as near as can be judged.—Author.

Bonur's studies and experiments were his one bright spot, to our eyes, but the truth was they led most often to a more painful, more darkly evil method of hurting something human— of making something far less than human out of flesh. They could not even begin to think of plans to replace the horror that ruled them, for the telaug beams of his cronies and slaves and favorites, always about, would have instantly revealed any such thought. Treachery could not have been repressed by a surface man, for every evil was in him, and a normal man cannot help desiring some rights, some dignity, some virtue to hold to with pride—something to cling to as an assurance that his life is not wholly a waste. But none of these were allowed under Bonur. To hold such thoughts was "treachery." Those who survived under Bonur assiduously cultivated a servility of mind, a thought-discipline of unimaginable severity of refusal of virtue, of unbelievable ferocity of lust for blood and death to anything that might threaten the supremacy of Bonur—and Satan.

And this mental attitude must be real, must always be worn like one's clothes, and must be followed as the rule of conduct upon all occasions. Those who failed to alter their soul to fit Bonur's nature—to fit it by scrupulous copying of that nature from observed activity of Lord Bonur—those people died slowly and in the eyes of all; a lesson to the rest.

BY CAREFUL suggestive work with the long range telaug by Brack and old Ben Uniaty, the mind of the cook had carefully been imbued with a complete fascination for the taste of the new condiment given him by the friendly stranger. The only precautions taken by Bonur against poisoning was a slave taster who must perforce take a bit of every kind of food and a sip of every drink before Bonur placed it in his mouth. Other than that Bonur and Nake had worked out a system of food supply for the Stem palace which made sure that every bit of food used in the palace was straight from the unconscious, unsuspicious surface food factories—brought direct by truck. But in the case of these feasts, in which human flesh was used, these precautions were necessarily relaxed.

That Bonur did not conceive of a slow poison that took effect long after the poisoning I can only attribute to his ignorance. He was an experienced man, an educated man as such go in the caves, but of wide learning of the kind dispensed by surface men he had none. For that matter, you would find upon search that many of our most powerful and hated men take few precautions against poison. It just seems to be a thing little done.

Bonur's youth and young manhood had been spent here in the Stem-palace; first as a child of an officer about the palace, later as a soldier, then an officer whose plotting had led at last to the leadership of a group of ray-warriors who had seized power by killing all those who stood in their way. That Bonur had got the throne had been due to his own ruthless killing of his confederates when the chance offered. For their part they were ignorant men, in our eyes—though in the underworld there is little education of a formal kind and a man's worth depends solely on the amount of skill he has been able to acquire with the varied kinds of antique ray-mech.

So it was that Bonur was great because his opportunities had proved great, due to the fact that his father and his friends had been in charge of the great vaults full of peculiar and terribly powerful devices stored by generations of acquisitive rulers of the Stem. Perhaps it was the greatest collection of powerful weapons and of antiques in the whole underworld. Bonur had supplied the know-how when the time for rebellion had come, and the vaults of the Stem had supplied the weapons. It had really been but a simple matter of disposing of a few trusted guards left in charge of the great vaults of the Stem's widespread, labyrinthine borings, the caves that made up the Stem-palace.

It is hard to understand how people with mechanisms to read minds either on the surface or in the caverns could be ignorant, but such is the case except in certain areas. They are either the hereditary rulers or children of wholly dependent slaves, or the free nomads of the deserted caverns. Originality, invention, courage of the mind, resourcefulness, ingenuity are qualities undeveloped among them because of the nature of their life, of the wholly different conditions of their world. It is best understood by considering India, which has perhaps had as much real opportunity to be a great modern nation as any; but has failed because of the repressive and smothering influence of its castes, its religions, its customs and its climate.

The cavern people are also a product of their environment, and that environment is a very different one from our own. That Brack or someone like him could slip a poison to his cook unobserved by the ever watching numerous telaug rays was unthought of by Bonur because it was considered impossible. It was in fact impossible to an ordinary man, but Brack and Tim were far from ordinary men. And Old Ben Uniaty was one of the wisest products of a life that has produced wizards since the pyramids. They were men who had made a lifetime study of ways of evading the objectionable forces in their life, and were perhaps the only men on earth who could have successfully fooled and evaded a ray-watch long enough to give Bonur's cooks the peculiar condiments under circumstances which would arouse no later pursuits, having left no trail in the minds of the men involved. The cook would not remember getting the poison, the thought-concealer device worn by Brack had successfully concealed his true thought with a superficial blanket of false thought as the deed was done, and now the thought in the cook's mind was wholly one of giving the food a much more appetizing flavor, rather than a thought of killing a great number of people in a wholesale poisoning.

IN THE Palace of the Stem the orgy of the Satanists is drawing to a close. The great robot statue of the Devil has danced ponderously, and the priestess has postured redly, her body glistening with the blood of the sacrifices, her lewd incantation to the God is finished, all the delights of sin depicted with a wealth of gesture.

The gloomy, crowded cavern is filled with smoke, with wine scents, perfume scents, blood scents, with the smell of sweat and unwashed bodies, with the odor of food and the roasted meats—and if one were on the lookout—the scent of the bag of peculiar and deadly drug acquired by Tim Shanter in the bedroom of the dead dancer Lura, mingling though well hidden by the other odors.

The lilies, red and black, which had been used to decorate the place lie now trodden into the straw on the floor. Half of the guests lie under the benches, too drunk to move.

In their hidden, imperviously sheathed den, Brack and the old man watch the progress of the feast elatedly. Nearly every one of the feasters has partaken of some of the poisoned meats. Bonur himself having come in for an hour to show his oneness with the pleasures of his things, to make sure that they are seated and comfortable and agreeable to his future plans. Red Nake was fed quite a bit of it by a charming slave girl, under Ben's suggestions, for Nake had not much appetite but could not resist the laughing girl.

As the last drunk was put to bed in the chambers adjoining the great feast hall, Tim Shanter piloted the old rollat containing Nita, Bill, Old Ben Uniaty and Brack farther and farther along the way leading to Bron, a small city some two hundred miles to the north of Ontal. They did not wish to be under the range of Bonur's ray beams as the poison began its long and painful course; a course of illness for which there was no cure, no known antidote—he might accidentally guess the source of his trouble before it killed him.

CHAPTER NINE
Red Nake's Revenge

THAT flight was a mistake. What ill-gotten goddess had put the thought in their minds? They were the only car on the roads that morning. This was not so unusual, but the empty-headed cook—whose mind's blankness had been their tool, now found his blundering way to becoming their inadvertent betrayer.

Nake was going over the kitchen stores totting up the cost of the feast. The cook, whose twenty-four hour memory had not had time to forget his suddenly acquired infatuation for the strange condiment given him by Brack, managed to find a moment to brag to Nake of the wonderful new flavoring for meats he had acquired. As he talked, Nake, listening contemptuously with half an ear, suddenly froze as the possibility of the thing flashed through his mind. For all of their stores of food were from the surface city. Not one iota of it was supposed to come from other sources than their own trusted agents. This custom had for long been one of their strongest safeguards against such an occurrence as the cook was glowingly outlining to Nake's suddenly fear-struck ears.

"For the sake of the Devil, let me see some of this marvelous flavor, you fat imbecile!"

The cook, foolishly not knowing it meant the loss of his life whether he showed him or not, promptly found the shaker of strange powder and gave it to Nake. Nake took it and raced off to Bonur's, but on the way a strange thought struck him and he stopped. If he could find out what was in it on his own; if it was poison; if there was an antidote; if he kept his big mouth shut— why the whole Stem would fall uninvited into his lap. He could take the antidote, slip it unnoticed to his favorite men, and stand back to watch the others curl up in death. It might be a bit of luck.

NAKE stood over the old chemist, a slave long a captive, but once a surface scientist of some renown. The old hands, shaking but still clever, poured reagent after reagent upon the powder.

"Seems to be everything under the sun in this mix. I can't tell what the poison is—if it is a poison—but I'll bet my last weeks food slips it *is*, and a little known one. This will take time, Nake. I never saw anything like this stuff, and I've seen a lot."

"There are some poisons that are found in the ancient's hidden stores, they would be hard to analyze and of substances unknown and hard to understand as to their effects. Is there any way you can tell me if this is a fatal dosage of poison in the amounts we got into us? There is not so much in the shaker and it was spread over quite a bit of meat."

The old chemist smiled at Nake and walked over to a goldfish bowl. He dropped a grain of the stuff in. For a few moments the fish swam as idly as ever about the bowl, but gradually their tails quivered faster and faster, they raced about the bowl for a long time, then turned belly-up, their bodies jerking with cramps. Finally they rose and lay on the surface but did not die, just lay there, gasping.

"It is a poison, Nake. It may act quite slowly on the human; the goldfish are very delicate and react to the slightest trace of a poison. What it is I do not know, but I will try to find out and tell you. I would suggest you find the men who gave it to you and learn from them the antidote if you can. It is a strange material."

As Nake left, the old chemist stood smiling absently after him. Once before he had been asked to analyze a very similar substance. A warm feeling rose within him and he suddenly cut a little caper with his feet as he realized that most of the devil-bunch at the feast must have got some of the stuff into them. He grinned steadily, breaking into low laughs as he returned to bed. There'd be little work he'd do finding an antidote. He might be old and slow, but not dumb.

NAKE hurried to his own quarters and woke two of his cronies. He set them to searching the city with the long telaug beams, searching every stray and curious thought for the slightest inkling of who might be responsible for the deed. Nake was rather explicit in telling them to keep their own mouths shut and minds guarded till they had learned whether or not the thing could be turned to account, or would prove the death of them.

So it was that as they swung the great old penetrays of the telaugs over the city of silence and despair the only moving thing in sight was the rollat bearing Brack and Tim, Nita and Bill and Old Ben. Their thoughts, though hidden by the devices Brack had hastily clapped about their heads, were still confusing and suspicious, for Brack in his hurry had not prepared a synchronized set of related records and the unrelated records showed a confusing mess of peculiar thought to the inquiring rays. Nake sent a police car racing after them on the chance that they might know something. There was something odd about their being the only car leaving the city.

THE five disheartened friends stood before Nake in his private quarters in the Palace of the Stem. Looking up at the great frowning faces of the carved Elder race; at the infinitely intricate parquetry of stone set in the walls in those designs no human could ever imitate; down at the purple glass of the floor where fishes of glittering gold and gleaming red and night black swam frozenly in the glistening glass; looking anywhere but at the eyes of Nake who had been poisoned, and wished mightily that he had been not poisoned.

He had swiftly found the thought-concealer record-mech they wore about their heads and removed them, put a beam from his own telaug upon each of their minds, was questioning them with a kindly smile on his face as though all this were but a joke, hoping to trap their startled minds into an admission of guilt—and succeeding. The telaug revealed the fact they had done the deed, but it also revealed that they themselves knew not the antidote for the dread, deadly stuff they had stolen from dead Lura's home.

Nake grinned a grim, evil smile of defeat at them as he listened to the slow, unwilling flow of their thoughts through the multi-screen before him. That screen could have carried a hundred separate beams from a hundred minds, if Nake had been man enough to read them all. But five were about as much as even his quick inner eye could follow.

Nake motioned to his friends, standing behind him with their ancient dis-pistols trained upon the five just in case the meek appearance of the five was not true. As Nake revealed the whole truth to their already alarmed minds, they snarled with rage, their fingers tightened on the huge triggers of the vastly oversize pistols. But Nake held up a hand to stay them, whispered again to them, and the fellow called Horr Bratt laughed such a laugh as a man reading his death sentence may laugh and hurried from the room.

"Just a little wine before I show you to your sleeping rooms." Nake's smile was as seductive as ever was Cleopatra's offering poisoned wine to a guest. Horr Bratt returned with a decanter of the blue grape, which he handed to Nake with a grimace of feigned pain, for he had already begun to imagine the pangs of what he knew must follow for him.

Nake took the decanter, lifted the stopper, and in plain sight of the five waiting silently he poured the full contents of the shaker the cook had given him into the mouth of the jug.

"It is an ancient potion that brings sweet dreams." Nake laughed at them again, and offered them glasses, which he filled.

"Drink, my friends, I have had enough wine for this night. And then to bed, to wait, for this potion brings sweet dreams, indeed! Unless, of course, you feel like talking, in which case we are quite willing to sit up with you, I'm sure. What would you have?"

As he stood in front of Bill, offering him the well-filled goblet of death, Bill reached his hand to the glass, took it and with the same motion flung it into Nake's face and dived for his legs. As they floundered on the floor, Nake snarled a word to Horr Bratt and the other not to kill.

"If you kill them, we will never learn the antidote!"

NAKE'S was a body well fed for long, while Bill was just recovering from the effects of months of slow starvation, the starvation that gripped the whole city under Bonur's merciless taxes. As Brack and Tim stepped forward to help him, Horr Bratt triggered two bolts into the glass floor, and great smoldering stars of cracks appeared in the glass under their feet. They stepped back; there was no way to help. They all felt doomed since they had been caught when all had seemed so safe, so well-covered and complete. Nake brought his pistol butt down on Bill's head and the struggle was over. Nake got to his feet snarling.

"No more foolishness, give us the antidote or drink your potion and go to sleep with it, as we must! You have no other course of action. A fool would know that dying men are not to be trifled with."

Ben Uniaty spoke in his oddly young voice that fit so ill with his time-ravaged face.

"We do not really know the antidote, Red Nake. If we did, we might be so foolish as to buy our lives with it. But as it is, here's to our lives in Paradise; sure you'll never reach there, Red Nake, with the crimes you have on your soul!"

Ben Uniaty, the best mind in all Ontal, drained the deadly potion and sat down, smiling oddly. Brack, hoping the old man had a card in the hole, but not seeing any other course open anyway, drained his own glass. Nita and Bill, looking at each other, drank theirs as though it were a love philter. Tim, the last, looked at his with the same dread that had plagued him in Lura's beauty-haunted home, finally managed to down it, grimacing. The five stood, facing Nake, as if to say, "What now, we are all dead; so what?"

"Take 'em away! They may remember later what to do about the stuff. Have them searched; some clue to an antidote might be concealed on them. Put them in separate cells, right here in this same boring. Post a guard at each door. It may be that one might crack and wish to bargain with us. The guards are to have strict orders to call us instantly one of them wishes to speak, understand!"

It was a sad blackness in which the friends waited. There was no hope, for none of them knew anything about the poison except that Lura had used it effectively. They were all glad they did not know an antidote, for it would have been wrested from their minds by the telaug and they would have died anyway. If they had been free, they might have searched Lura's effects, found some trace of the antidote. But they knew that Nake had read in their minds where the stuff had come from and had sent a search party there himself. They knew that if the antidote were found, themselves would get none, and their death be more sure.

THE little slave-girl, Sarah, swung her watch-ray from Nake's apartments and upon the bed of Bonur where he snored loudly. A secret and somehow beautiful smile played over her childishly sweet face as she resolved to say nothing. For in the time that Ben Uniaty had focused the teleport upon the chair where Bonur was removing her mind and replacing it with his own design, Ben had found time to subtly insert a beam of invisible "shorter" ray which had reduced the power of Bonur's erasing ray to near zero. So that Sarah's treatment had lasted but a few days. And now Sarah was again Sarah! Bending over the screened image of Bonur she watched him, vengefully grateful that the death stuff was in him, watching for the first signs of its effects upon him. Already she noted his limbs twitch with the first tremors of the approaching painful convulsions.

Outside, the great stone faces of the mighty God-wrought stone figures that lined the way of the Stem looked wisely at each other, saying, "Wisdom is death, tonight. All is death and forgotten greatness, tonight."

Two weeks dragged by on slow, but fiery feet.

CHAPTER TEN
Death, King of Ontal!

ABOUT the palace of the Stem, and on the ways leading out of Ontal, were some thousands of things in human form, and of those thousands most were beginning to feel the pangs of a strange disease—a fire of pain began to spread through their limbs and convulse their muscles.

On the ways leading out of the city, the rollats, big as circus vans and some as ornate—though with the antique decoration that is never anything but exquisite—were parked beside the wide tubes in the alcoves that the ancients built at intervals. Inside, the devil ray-men writhed their small and twisted bodies in the first pangs of the long road to death they would all travel.

Inside the palace of the Stem, Bonur awoke, his whole body bathed in sweat in his dreams—which his slave watchers provided always in his sleep—had been strangely filled with foreboding. He had dreamed that the golden robot girl, the prophet machine the mad wight had brought from the south, had risen from the melting pot and came in to him, her terrible, musical voice telling him that soon, now, he would die!

Now, as he lay there in the luminous dark, Sarah's face bending over him in ray projection seemed the face of the terribly beautiful prophetess of doom—the golden girl herself. Slowly, the fearful fire of the pain from Lura's antique poison began to run through his veins, and Bonur felt such fear as he never had before. He leaped from the antique metal bed, as wide as three and as long as four, on which his spreads of silk and wool lay like a pallet on a giant's table, and rang a gong beside the bed. The obsequious slave who answered he sent to fetch Nake and Horr Bratt, for these two were in his closest counsel. Bonar divined that all was not well, and that he needed a doctor.

Nake came in all long-faced and gloomy, and answered Bonur's questions.

"I guess some enemy has got to us, Chief! I caught the cook right after the feast with some strange flavor in a box, and I have been having it analyzed and chasing hither and thither about it, not knowing whether it was nothing or a something to bother you about—and now the pains begin. I guess it wasn't all lies about Lura killing long after she gave them poison. It's over two weeks since the feast, and now it shows up. I guess there really are poisons that can kill long after the time you take them."

But of the captured, under guard in his own apartments, he said nothing, for it was too late to be caught with them on his hands and not have told Bonur.

Bonur swore.

"Then there was poison at the feast? I'll burn the lives out of every rat in Ontal till I get the one that did it. I'll kill every child till the parents tell what this is…I'll…"

Bonur's voice died, and he sat and stared, the pains running through him. For once he had come up against something he could not cure by killing someone.

"Nake, get every doctor in Ontal here. We'll get to the bottom of this if we have to burn the feet off everyone of them. We'll get some pill roller that knows something about this."

"I'll get 'em, never fear. I have the boys out rounding up all the talent of the kind. We'll soon have every pill-roller in the city at work on finding out what it is we have got into us."

"If we had a sample…"

Nake produced the shaker and handed it over.

"Here is the stuff, chief, someone gave this to the cook with a wool about it being the best flavoring the world has ever seen, and the simpleton swallowed the yarn hook, line, and sinker. He is in bed now, having tasted the stuff long before it got into the food, but the poison is so slow of working that it is only beginning to get him down. By the looks of him he'll live a week or two yet. We may have three weeks, maybe one, it depends on how much of the stuff we got into us."

TIME passed on painful, burning feet in the Palace of the Stem, and on the ways leading out of Ontal. It was now three weeks since the poison had been administered and all the victims were weakened by the effects. The "pill-rollers" worked night and day, might and main, in the great empty laboratory of the Stem; where once had been scientists with an education in some ways better than surface technologists, but now for years had been no one.

The symptoms, which had at first been slight recurrent pains, had increased daily in severity and pain and frequency. Now, three weeks after, from Bonur down to the lowliest lackey—and the innocent cook, causative tool—on down to the lowest mad denizen and devotee; all writhed and screamed day and night from the fires that consumed their lives so painfully, so slowly, so mysteriously.

In the cells in Nake's quarters, where the five conspirators waited Nake's torture—which occurred necessarily between his spasms of pain and increased in severity in proportion to his own agony—hope had left them. But a fierce pride in knowing they had freed Ontal of her worst oppressors upheld them.

The hardest thing for them to bear was the torture of Nita. For they had to witness what was done to her, hear her poor screams, watch her flesh torn with the whip—all the intricate engines of torment which the endless centuries of devil worship had passed down to these modern devotees of the red horned One. All were practiced before their eyes on poor Nita's shrieking beauty to wring from them the secret of the antidote. Yet all the time Nake knew it was hopeless, for in their minds could be read by his telaug experts the clear fact that they did not know of any antidote, if one existed. So that as his own pains increased steadily in severity, Nake gave up the hopeless job and left the poor wracked victims alone in their cells, while he devoted his rapidly waning energies to flogging on the efforts of the technicals he had called in to find the antidote by chemical means.

He promised tremendous rewards if they succeeded, but as neither he nor Bonur had bothered much with paying anyone for anything since they had got power in Ontal, these promises only served to remind the workers that their work was more or less a gift.

The dying ray-watch, who read the minds of the workers frantically trying reaction after reaction upon the sample of stuff they had, knew the case was hopeless unless some lucky chance should reveal a clue to their eyes. For they had no idea what many of the ingredients of the material were, and Ben's efforts to disguise the odor of the stuff beneath a multitude of flavors and odors had complicated their job till the Devil himself could not have told what it was.

AT LAST came the hour when the sentry before Bill's cell door collapsed shrieking at his post. His legs, kicking in the last throes of death, were just beyond their reach. Escape was open to them, if they had the keys. They lay beyond Bill's stretching pain-wracked arm and out of reach of Nita's own futilely reaching, lash-scored hands.

But out of his own agony Bill drew a last brief strength of mind, and tearing his cell cot apart, made a hook of metal out of the spring. Tugging, fainting, reaching, at last he brought the key ring from the belt of the fallen guard to his own hands.

Bill, knowing he was doomed, and that there was no point in his actions, automatically unlocked the cell door, and staggering from weakness, unlocked the cell doors of the others. Old Ben Uniaty lay apparently lifeless in the bed within the cell. Bill shook him savagely, not with hope, but because any action seemed to ease the terrible fire that consumed his veins, his life.

He picked up the old man, and, leading the others, who supported each other, led the way from the hated place. At least they might die at home, among loved surroundings.

As they fell and staggered down the great two-foot steps outside the palace of the Stem, to the round at the side of the way where were parked a mass of vehicles whose drivers would never again pilot them through the dark but weird and awfully beautiful ways of time-forgotten Ontal, old Ben Uniaty managed to murmur:

"To my laboratory, to the great metal room where my workshop lies, I may have remedy for the poison. Hurry, man, hurry!"

Bill surmised the old man was out of his mind—as indeed he appeared to be at the last threshold of consciousness—but decided to please his last wish anyway, though himself wanted to see his own loved chamber of the sculptured sea-plants and supremely beautiful females of the forgotten race in the stone niches where the water poured over them greenly forever; the room that his love for Nita had made sacred. Still Bill turned the wheels of the rollat toward Ben's workshop deep in the bowels of the city.

When they arrived, Bill had to carry the unconscious bodies of his friends into the place one by one, for none of them could more than murmur and weakly lift their arms to aid him. Within, himself collapsed across the body of Brack.

And the great enigmatic machines that Ben alone knew the slightest possible use for seemed to stare sadly at the five fallen there before them. And a spirit was in the room weeping, the spirit that was the soul of Ontal, for here lay her best, her bravest—and if there was hope in the old man's mind, there was none here, for his hands were fast stiffening in death.

Time dragged her weary, solemn feet through the great metal room, and the reward of their effort for the great future life of man was to be denied them. And something that men know, but never see, wept silently as the seconds ticked off the last breaths of five who tried nobly for their brothers, and paid the cost in full.

Bill, after long moments, lifted his head and his glazing eyes fell on one of the great machines that crowded there in the safety of the impervious metal walls. And that machine was one he had known in his infancy. On his hands and knees he crawled, inch by slow inch, to the feet of the metal monster, and pulling himself upright at last, turned the great metal stud that gave it power. Within the enigma that such ancient things always are to all men, power hummed a song, and from the bowl that was its face a flood of strange energy poured strength into Bill. For Bill would have to be nearer dead than he was not to recognize a beneficial ray mech when he saw it. Such rays are the coveted and valued possession of all who live and survive in the caves, for life is not supported in the darkness without these rays to replace our sun's less detrimental and necessary rays.

As new strength flowed into him, Bill raised and looking at the grey head and knowing old Ben would be the first to finally succumb to the effects of the poison, dragged the old man under the vibrant light of the powerful ben-mech. Bill then crawled again to Nita's side, took her dress in his teeth, and began dragging her into the light. As her body lay at last within the vibrant, rosy light of the ben-ray, his will exhausted its last reserve power, the floods of pain from the fire in his vitals washed over him. Darkness again wrapped him.

WITHIN the great gloomy Palace of the Stem, death reigned. The guards lay stiffened at their posts; in the harems and slave quarters the soft bodies of the women lay sprawled here and there and here and there one twitched and moaned until the death rattle silenced the moans.

In Nake's rooms, under the strong beneficial rays of his private mech, lay Nake, alone now, groaning, writhing and cursing, but still very much alive thanks to the life-generating power of the dynamos of the ben-ray mech.

On the great God-throne, so ludicrously too large for this contorted, bloated body, within his throne room in the Stem-palace, sprawled Bonur Golz. His eyes stared at the shadows deepening around him. Up the great steps of the dais, stealthily, silently, crept Sarah, his slave-girl, a ray gun huge in her soft hands. Sarah was weak, near death, but on her livid face her so-long obscured will flamed in that spirit that drove Joan of Arc.

Up to Bonur's twitching, contorted, bloating body she crept silently as the shadow of death itself. Bonur looked up to see her face, distorted with the hate she bore him, and to hear her say: "Just to make sure, Bonur Golz, my love! Pah! Toad, die!"

The great dis-ray pistol held out in her two shaking hands spit a brilliant bolt of terrible energy through Bonur's fat belly, through the mighty stone of the great throne, through the far wall.

She slipped to the floor beside the terrible dignity of the God throne, and the scene of her last deed in life did honor even to that awesomely sculptured chamber of ancient honor and striving. For Sarah strove in her hate, and died so, trying to do right. The gross horror crouched on the God throne was dead, and the sculptured faces looked down on Sarah as she died with their stony approval not incongruous. The spirit of the Elder race lives on in the human and as long as there are Sarahs there will be men worthy to carry on the striving toward the ancient greatness.

BACK in old Ben Uniaty's workshop, the old man lifted his grey head weakly under the full power of the great ben-ray mech. He looked wearily at the sprawled, still bodies of his friends about him—and full consciousness came and looked out of his eyes, fast glazing as they were in death.

Then the will that had driven him so long to fight when all seemed hopeless; fight so hard that all Ontal mistook him for the moving spirit of that great organization, the "helpers," raised him to his knees, made him crawl in spite of death already stiffening his limbs toward the huge levers manipulating the teleport mech. His shaking, enfeebled hands pulled the great lever, and majestically the terrific enigma of the teleport rose gleaming from its hiding bath of mercury. It rose and stood like the Godhead of all machine-heaven before him.

Into the focus chamber he crawled, turned the dial, and the terrible power whined as the complex multi-beam filled the room. And Ben Uniaty was sent by the teleport mech for a distance of six feet—as had been his yearly custom for many years.

He lay exhausted for long minutes, for the soul tearing experience of the titanic forces controlled by the machine had taken the last part of his nearly vanished strength.

Then his slow crawl began again, and Brack lay at last within the focus chamber. Again the dials and the big switches clicked, and Brack too lay some feet further away. Now Ben began again his crawl and strength was slowly returning to him. Though his breath came in great gasps, at least, it came.

Ben Uniaty loved men, and he knew that if he could teleport each of his dying friends the exclusion set-up of the titanic force-fields of the mighty teleport mech would leave the toxic material of the poison that was killing them outside their bodies in the sending chamber.

Ben Uniaty won, and the five friends, refreshed, but weak—after a long night's sleep under the great old beneficial rays—got ready to return to the Stem-palace. Out into the ever-night of ancient Ontal, toward the palace, Tim Shanter swung the great rollat's wheels, and a grim smile was on his face as he said:

"This day Ontal acquires a new ruler, yourself, Ben Uniaty, the best man in all the underworld!"

Inside the Palace of the Stem, Nake the Red gave a last groan, and as he expired under the strong beneficial ray that had failed to stop the poison death, Nake saw a strange face peering at him. Nake's last sight on earth was the face of a despised thief of the city who spat in his face and went on with his looting.

THE END

LETTER TO READER:

After reading over this story, I find that my attempt to give the true flavor of the underworld has not resulted very happily, insofar as speech is concerned. They speak several dialects of English. I have heard an old ruler telling his dream maker in these words:

"Shew me the hand. Shew me the foot. Shew me the waist and the movement therein, shew me the lust in her mind." Such English, I assure you, is impossible of reproduction unless you have been raised with it. Again, they use a jargon of slang more peculiar to themselves than jitterbug talk to the jitterbug—a modern slang—but the terms of it are full of words of double and triple meaning I have no power to put into English. If I tried to write entirely as it is you might refuse the whole thing. So I hope you will bear with the crudities I find I have committed for the sake of the story's vital information I give those who already know enough of the hidden world to know I give them much.

Your friend,
Richard S. Shaver.

AFTERWARD TO
"THE MASKED WORLD"

HERE I think I should give you the gist of a newspaper clipping I have before me (clipped from either the *Sun* or the *Herald American* of Chicago, of approximately September 27, 1945—I do not recall the exact date as I clipped it a week ago and do not have the original paper; but if you are interested in checking me, the item should be easily found). The clipping gives the following general information:

"A young lady in Chicago (whose name and address I shall not mention to save her still further embarrassment—Shaver) has complained to the U. S. District Court that the Federal Bureau of Investigation is guilty of what she terms "malfeasance of duty" in permitting her to be troubled by rays, electric shocks, voices and radio eyes.

"In filing her own suit, the young lady complained that she had informed the FBI about her troubles but they had done nothing about it. (They couldn't—Shaver) She attributed the rays, voices, eyes and shocks to "un-American interests paving the way for anarchistic rule in this country." (They are always going to "come to the surface" and take over our government—they never do!—Shaver)

"Naming Newark, NJ" as the place where her troubles began, she said: "There was some sort of equipment held in the rear of another residence, which could vibrate the building, or the bed in which I attempted to sleep." (There is some of the antique mech on the surface, brought up.—Shaver)

"Later, she moved to Wheeling, W. Va. But the rays followed her there. The FBI, she said, compelled her to sit under and over some sort of heat, whether it was radium lamps or other heat she did not know.

"In Chicago she asked that the court compel the FBI to solve the mystery and uncover these secret rays that were bedeviling her."

There you have the gist of the clipping, which is only one of thousands of clippings in a like vein that appear yearly in American newspapers. Their source is quite obvious to one who knows.

Many, many people like this unfortunate woman are sent to the madhouse every year for maintaining such "ridiculous" assertions. It gets in the papers—and there is so much of it that I believe an outfit as big as the FBI must know a great deal about the causes of these phenomena. It is most probable that they have found themselves helpless against such things, but if so their attitude in allowing their silence on the subject to send sane people to the madhouse is hard to understand. Perhaps they have their reason—they fear the panic results of exposing their information to all surface men.

But for those of you who do not intend to go to court and courageously hold the whole cave menace up to the light of day and spur the FBI in this particular endeavor to publicize one of the most evil farces in modern life—I have written the following story. It will explain just what is behind such news items.

For instance such a news item as the following—started me on this story because I felt guilty as hell for the death of seventeen service men, because I know more or less the real cause of the wreck and fail convincingly to acquaint the general public with the facts that would enable them to take *some* measures for their safety.

Remember the night of August 10? I was sitting by the radio, deep in the work of another stf. writer—when the radio gave the news with which I began this manuscript; the item concerning the wreck of the Great Northern Empire Builder in Michigan, North Dakota.

It was this radio announcement that made me get up and go at my typewriter, resolved to lift the veil that hides the idiot evil that causes such wrecks once and for all. This story is the result. It is basically true, all the parts are true existent things. But the assembly as a whole is fiction. The "Stem" exists, but I am not sure whether it is under New York or a certain other great city. There are only three or four such great entrances; the rest are closed.

YOU have read descriptions of the ancient slave marts? You have seen them in the movies, certainly. But did you know that the ancient slave market is an institution that has not died? That it lives on and flourishes in secret; as so many other ancient evils live on and flourish in secret and also in the concealment and protection of the caves; protected not only by the natural barriers of the miles of dense granite and basalt above, but also by the unmatched weapons of the Pagan God race themselves?

Depending wholly on these protective "shells," the animal "man" seems to have evolved very differently—or not at all. He must be seen to be understood. Inheriting absolute power as well as numbers of sycophants from their fathers, the rich and powerful—like the Rajahs of Indian history—are often weak, bloodthirsty, dissipated, wholly characterless (though I have seen the reverse), wholly a burden to their people. And this is a particularly terrible problem when their weapons are so invincible. Even to the sane, well-intended of the caverns who know the immensely technical field of antique ray mech operation intimately, it is also an insuperable problem, for weapons to defeat the antique stationary ray installations just aren't portable because of weight.

Tortures are a large part of the life of these evil ray of the caverns, and I will list a few of the more common things you must face to have a piece of the antique mech to study.

"Flaying alive."—Burning over a fire while being simultaneously whipped with a heavy metal-thonged whip.

"The steam chair"—a particularly delightful death much feared by the persecuted peoples of the underworld. It is a chair built of metal tubes into which live steam is admitted after the victim has been thoroughly lashed in place.

A favorite method of torture much used because the victim can survive to be sold as a slave, if care is used, is "freezing." By means of specially constructed devices shaped for the purpose built of refrigerating units, the victim is frozen solid over and over. The freezing is not particularly painful, but the "thawing out" is excruciating agony. After a few such treatments one is either dead or ready for any vileness asked of one—or such is the theory behind much of the torture; though to my knowledge few survive these entertaining ordeals.

To top the unpleasant aspects of the life of the caverns, many of the slaves are eunuchs, likewise many of the female slaves are brutally sterilized.

Some are given "stim-death" just for the fun of watching the nerve impulse augmented electrically until it is the power of a well-nigh-killing electric shock. The victim kills himself by too violent contortions of the body. The back breaks or the arms break in the thongs, or the legs break in the anklets, and the victim bleeds to death.

Another favorite is the sclerosing solution in the veins. Plain Lysol is often used.

THE SHAVER MYSTERY, Book Three

WHEN the owners pass in to the slave market with their slaves, the guard at the entry gate cries:

"State your stock."

The owner then enumerates the number and sex and age of his slaves. Inside, one hears such snatches of conversation as this: "He just practically gave away two kids." (Two children sold cheaply).

"Now she's on sale." *She* is a beautiful and cultured young American girl from the surface. She brings a good price from an old "crackpot."

Or: "And the market price in children is rising since the use of young blood transfusions for rejuvenation is in style."…"One's own child is apt to become a blood-cow for some old jerk to get young. And I'm supposed to be loyal! The least bad luck, a bum steer, a wrong gamble, and my own kids go to the block to become blood-cows for these dirty medical ray groups to sell to some rich old geezer!"…"Speak of torture, I saw a new one on my last trip into the territory of that whirligig witch, Nonur. She had acid grease prepared and smeared all over the flesh of a young fellow. What a prolonged torment! The grease slows and prolongs the acid action; the flesh rots away."…"Yeah, it gets worse and worse. The green (money) is never enough. The price on young blood rises. One's sweat is never rewarded, while the fools and cheats, the double-crossing sneaks prosper. When you find a wise man, you find a man who lives in torment from the mad ray. A dream is never good, but is always perverted by some tampering dero into a nightmare. Love is turned phony in your arms by the stim ray. The only laughter you hear is a stupid, evil cachinnation, and never anymore a real laugh of joy. Whatever a guy wants or could enjoy, it's 'all.' If you ask for credit it's as good as asking for jail."

This is a short picture of the cave life to show you Shaver's answer to the readers' rather frequent query: "Why doesn't Shaver lead a party into the caves?" *I'm* willing, but which

179

entrance opens into a safe place where such a state of affairs is not waiting to engulf us?

Slavery of our best and most beautiful seems to be the actual case under some areas of our country. I have laid my picture of the actual, terrible life of the people of the caverns under New York, not because such is the case there (though to my knowledge it is *not* good there), but because the name will make you realize that all is not as it appears with American life. Much of this is concealed by corruption and intimidation of the personnel of our census and missing persons bureau. If you don't believe me, try and prove differently. You will probably find missing persons personnel "out to lunch." The "ray" receives large sums from various surface groups seems very true, for their lavish expenditures could only be so explained, or by the possession of many gold mines in the deeper caves. That many people do disappear into the complete slavery in the caves is obviously true if you know anything at all about the cavern life. The police obviously fear to admit where they go or even that they do go; that there are continual and unexplained disappearances every day (or in truth do not know either!). That these are hidden in never-referred-to files of records is obviously true.

THE well-stocked harems and slave pens of some of the big-shots underneath are obviously the big reason why the caverns are still the same ancient, secret, and powerful influence in our lives they have always been.

Naturally I can't take people into a place where they would become beaten slaves—and the first taste of slavery they would get would be the lash, for they would object to becoming slaves. Truth is, it is possible to get into and out of the caves without this sad fate; but it takes money in equipment and attendant publicity to cause the underworld to leave it alone for fear of exposing their hand.

Down there, the leases and contracts are written in "vanishing" ink; and when you are broke, you are sold as a slave to cover your debts.

You see, they are a slave state and an absolute and terrible tyranny bordering our free surface states. When you enter you become a slave, your property confiscated by the most powerful native you encounter.

The rulers are sometimes descendants of a long line of rulers. They are people who have always lived thus and see no reason for change. Tyranny is their way of life.

When a slave becomes useless, it is as at Oswiecim, and the other German murder camps. He is disposed of as cheaply as possible. In the caves he is thrown in "the hole"—down and down his body goes, still screaming from his last torment. No man knows where such holes go into the depths.

To really describe the life of the caverns is beyond words. We do not have the concepts or the experience with evil life to understand what is true when we read it. But I can try!

They fear and obstruct all scientists on the surface with the ancient penetrative rays that reach up and watch us through the miles of rock that protects them from our knowledge—and from our vengeance when, like Shaver, men know what they do. Such men as Pierre Curie almost always die strangely; and must always so die as long as the caverns roam with the mad nomads, or the cities of the surface are underlaid with the sinks of sin which do exist there. He must die as if it was an accident and he does. Like Pierre he walks into a loaded truck obliviously, and is crushed. Or like Seabrook—who knew more than he dared tell—take sleeping tablets not because they want to, but because they are made to by rays controlling their bodies.

The people who do this did not build these rays, but they have learned how to use them and have kept the use secret in the endless centuries that have passed since the caves became tabu to surface men (except as slaves, and in some places—as food).

The evil groups of the underworld—which is in some places the only areas of earth where stupid, evil and backward men hold power since Hitler's death and Japan's surrender—fear all scientific progress up here. Hence their dog-in-the-manger attitude toward surface technicians acquiring even one piece of the indestructible antique mech. In the hands of quite a few surface men—hex-doctors of Pennsylvania; witch-doctors of Africa; seers and spiritualists; fortune tellers; criminals—are samples of the antique mech and they are used but are never turned over to surface technicians to study because of the ancient tradition of secrecy. The influential ones of the underworld are often backward mentally, culturally, technically, and spend their lives' powerful efforts trying to hold back, to make the surface world "wait" till they catch up with us mentally and technically. But they do not in truth progress down there, and so this is an endless struggle.

THIS story Masked World is a courageous attempt to picture this world under our feet for you as nearly as may be done with words and ideas which are not adapted to portraying concepts you are not used to as "true" concepts. The speech they use is hard to reproduce, for they use so much telaug meaning, double meaning, that their English would not be understood by you unless you heard it mentally. Orally it does not reproduce.

It is not a "fine" story, and it might be frowned upon by ignorant moralists of the type who teach our young that all is sweetness and light in the world except for minor details which are being "tended to" by our FBI and kindred agencies. It doesn't do what I want, portray the full truth of the life of the underworld. But as an attempt in that direction you will find it valuable. It does give you some idea of what goes on under your feet in the ever-night of the caverns where the forgotten Gods built their mighty cities before earth ever had a sun—deep in the rock where even the super-cold of space could not reach. We cannot reach or harm these people below us, but they do a good job of ruining their own life, if that is what you think should happen to those who deny surface people the products of an elder culture that would give us a future beyond the power of words to describe. Most of the parts of this story are actual true occurrences, but the assembly as a whole is, of course, fiction. And for those who can't stand the idea that such things *can* be true—it is a clever concoction of lies.

Since the story is designed to give you a complete picture of life in the Masked World under our feet, it is not complete without the inclusion of a few of the incidents that make up the life of the mad, sadistic nomads who forever infest the wonderland that their dog-in-the-manger attitude denies to our eyes—and of the science which would make surface medicine a wonder of perfection in its fight against disease. These madmen below us deny our right to that health that the secrets of the old mech would give us. They are things which evil men use for their purpose, too stupid to want proper recompense or ask for it; things, which the sane avoid like the plague, down there, or kill on sight if they are able, if their ray reaches them first.

And these same things of the "netherworld" (familiar phrase to a student, eh?) have been used by surface people in the past (called "witches" and worse) for their own purposes. Since in those days not many of them had a spoken language, and in truth there were probably too few of them survived the darkness—for to survive the darkness one must have certain kinds of rays containing ultra-violet always upon one's body— they could only be communicated with by signs. This was an art that some families learned from their parents and kept secret, for to talk of it was to die as a witch. When they hated someone, or wanted someone removed for some purpose, all they had to do was to go to a secret place, make a doll resembling the person hated, and stick pins in the doll. The watching ray from below noted what was wanted from the appearance of the doll and promptly stuck the real person with very real and deadly rays from the ancient weapons that abounded around him. So, we have the legend of the doll of the witches (witch-craft) in full explained! It was a result of a very real and deadly code in use between the underworld and the surface.

What did the surface witch give for such a service? She gave her body over the stim-telaug at any time desired—and on Walpurgis Night gave it in full, in an even more actual form. Such was the sale of the soul to the devil; and in many cases I doubt very much that it was evil at all. But in many cases it was evil, and no mistake about it. In my own case it was not evil. But I know well how much evil there is still there, and what it was in medieval and ancient times one can well imagine. I have nearly lost my life to such evil several times, and I still worry. But the thing known as "white magic" in the old days, and as the "helpers" today, always intervened in time. One's effort has a value still in the underworld, it seems.

THERE are an infinitude of legends and detailed accounts of this communication between the magical underworld and the humdrum surface world. But those "not in the know" have always insisted that all such tales were lies; and usually have been ably assisted in this shutting of themselves off from a very profitable communion by those who did know all about it.

I can imagine the first shouted "bosh" when the yokel started to tell of the opening he had found leading down to "fairyland" belonged to a gentleman who is still with us, the mountebank and charlatan who uses the underworld to his nefarious ends.

It was the gentleman who told fortunes at the fair, or the gambler who used the underworld wights clever ray work to tell what cards his friend held across the board—and who got this very profitable and frequently very able work for the mere running of a few errands to places where their peculiar appearance barred the underworld from entrance without recognition or apprehension as minions of the Devil. He didn't want his life's sweetest bounty ruined by some yokel's foolish revelation.

There are such individuals shouting "bosh" at *Amazing Stories* today, and they know more about it than we do—and get much more out of it! There are others who think the underworld is wholly their friend—and those are the first to shout "bosh" at such as me. But there is too much evil rising out the old place, and it is time we took a hand in Hell's hotter brews of evil. They cost too much in blood and tears, those mad and evil ones. All the kindhearted "white magic" in the world does not make up for it. They need a large hand, a helping hand, and those good ones below. In one state, one day, lately, ten sane men were committed to the madhouse as incurably mad. Their minds had been deluded by the mischievous cruelty of the more evil subterranes into a state that no psychiatrist could see as anything but mad. Truth was, they had been treated to a few depressions of the buttons on an emotion organ, a few projections of real seeming phantasms from the telesolidograph mech, and had gone screaming out of their minds. They would be all right in a few days, but once in an insane asylum they would not be released for months to come. Truth is, you can't tell many medics a story like this as true without their calling the wagon. "It just couldn't be!" But you see, it is true, so it must be told.

Seabrook, a writer and investigator of the reason behind witchcraft and other weird phenomena of life, died at his farm in Rhinebeck on September 20, 1945. The doctor found him dead from an overdose of sleeping pills. But Seabrook had been deviled by rays for years. The sleeping pills were taken by him under ray control, for the old ray mech is an ideal tool that can take over a man's body in such a way that all his acts are dictated by thought superimposed upon his brain in such strength that his own thought has no power over his actions. Such was Seabrook's death. The truth is Seabrook knew the truth, but had been unable to publicly say so for fear of the madhouse. Many men are in that position.

THE Satanists' banquet was men like Bonur's tool, back into the beginnings of life on earth; their means of getting the evil ones of the cavern into an illusion of loyalty, of receiving compensation for their efforts. They are not gifted with brains, being in truth an idiotic form of life, which the peculiar conditions of the cave life had fostered in some areas for ages. The life support given by the magnificent machinery of maintaining life under all conditions left by the ancients had succeeded only in perpetuating a kind of life that could exist only in these ultra-favorable conditions. They were wholly evil, and the errors of their ways never were corrected by nature, for the ancient beneficial rays and weapons allowed them to survive when better men perished. The truth is, the machinery had removed all need for effort from their lives and the result had been a degeneration of a most repellent kind—and as the truth is that evil is a reverse form of logic, they were supremely stupid for they had never found a real need for thought; it had all been done for them by the Gods who left the caverns to them.

The custom of using these evil degenerates as a cheap kind of assassin had become an institution of cavern life. They were paid little or nothing, but their evil natures had to be pandered to and coddled in certain ways, as they were irritable and unstable unless so treated. The annual feast of the Satanists had thus grown into an age-old part of their life, and was one way of keeping them in hand. Each year it was almost an exact repetition of the year before. The minds of the dero, if they can be said to have minds, were not such as to require much change in the fare. The dances of the red-masked figures were an exact and changeless repetition of some ritual so old its origin was as lost in time as the origin of the Elder race itself.

During the great Feasts of the Demons, one of the songs the devils hear contains these words in a tune familiar to you as a hymn—but known for centuries in the caverns as a song of the Demon's triumph over aspiring surface man:

"Twill be my Demon's glory...
Jesus on the cross...

The words are distorted version of one of our much used hymns, and tells the story of the demon who connived and controlled the Romans and the Jews until Jesus was finally dying on the cross. I have often wondered since I first heard the Demon's hymn whether our hymn was first written or was a present, a mocking gift, from the underworld so that we might sing our dupe's hymn to a deed they hold as one of their mightier stunts, an incident in their long reign of terror over all earth, a reign they have upheld by frustrating all man's attempts toward union in good sensible effort toward a sane goal of humane power on earth.

THE eating of the flesh of a baby was considered an essential part of the ceremony. The custom had been curtailed by time till but one babe was usually slaughtered before the red idol, cut into small pieces and partaken of each as a symbol of the individual's emancipation from all human emotions, and of his complete prostration before the spirit of evil.

The Demon is not a figment of man's imagination; they have been a strong organization always, and today are perhaps as strong or more so than ever and as big a force in life. They have their hymns, and many of them are the very hymns we sing in our Christian churches—but they are older and the words are often the horrible original from which our own hymns were given us in mockery. I have heard these hymns sung to the "god" of evil, and the antiquity of man's prostration and help-lessness before these evil latter Gods who have duped and bedeviled man and held him back from his destiny by the evil teaching that they themselves were not men but demons—is the saddest history I have ever encountered.

The dero have been man's curse and are the reason man is mortal and worthless today. One cannot tell in words the terrible stretch of evil antiquity that can ring in the words of a demon's song. If I could but remember the words for you; it is a glimpse into the horror that is a race's madness through time, the demon race—the race that became devils because the machines they worshipped became sun-polared.

I think that this occurred in this way: The cavern dwellers have a way of warming and cheering their gloomy homes by turning a conductive ray up through the rock and by it bringing the sun's rays themselves into the cavern over the penetrative conductive ray. Then when the sun set, they were as apt as not to use the same mech for making dreams, for the versatility of mech is often many such devices in one. I have seen them do this—use a dream machine, which is really the old record reader—the library of thought record's necessary adjunct without which the old thought records could not be read. But the dream-mech, as the cavern people call them, had also a penetrative ray by which the record pictures could be thrown to great distances. The same machine, because of the nature of this ray designed to convey the most subtle and variant of thought waves in their entirety, also served as the best ray to bring the light of the sun into the caves. So it was that the dream-mech became sun-polared.

In time they came to use the same mech for the making of dreams—which is a way of using the record reader to produce dreams—for in the record-mech is a way of introducing one's *own* thought to the person receiving the record so that one's wildest fancies can be introduced into the fabric of the story of an ancient recording of the thought of an ancient elder man. This may be difficult to follow, but the wise ones of the modern dwellers below have told me that this is the way the demon originated on earth. His mind became sun-polared from the radioactive machine, which had become so by exposure to long periods to the direct rays and inductive power of the sun itself. So it was that the mad sun-inductive mind of the demon was inevitable—for they had to have sunlight—and the means by which they got sunlight became the means of evil's domination of their lives.

So it was that the demon became a hereditary character dominating the cavern life; and today the same danger threatens and destroys and may wipe out surface life again as it has done before, over and over. History is not all in history books, you see.

TO GET back to the feast of the devils repeating its age-old pattern of evil under hands like Bonur's grasping hand—the red masks, the black robes, the details you are familiar with from your Christian descriptions of Hell—were here seen for what they were in truth, an "actual" thing of living, degenerate people of a race that had lost its birthright of reason from an affliction peculiar to their uses of the ancient machines for centuries after they had become unfit for use—their ignorance of the science behind the wonder-mech giving them no inkling of the fate the sun-polared mech would doom them to—the fate of degenerating into inhuman, unthinking, and complete demoniac creatures.

In the past these creatures have emerged from the caverns and swept all life from the vast areas of earth's surface; and their wide dispersion under earth has succeeded in their mad single-minded secretive destruction of records of their past in keeping all knowledge of the origin and nature of evil from us of the surface. This condition is what I have set myself to remedy—and this story is my vehicle to this purpose. So I hope you will bear with me if I have diverged from the story form, for the task is a great one, and I fight not only ignorance but a complete inheritance of obstructing thought which is our own heritage of stupidity from the past influence of the demon's fingers forever in our minds in the ages past.

For instance if I try to tell you the awful depths of the degradation of human-like things who had degenerated so many centuries in dark destructive secrecy under our feet, the ignorant man who is in position to stop such revelations imagines I am transgressing the law of morality, even though my purpose is wholly to depict evil as it really is so you may know it.

Yet the dark heritage of ours steps in shouting "lewd", "must be censored" etc. So if I omit the details of this debauch as I know it to be—you must allow for these obstacles and supply the revolting details from your own imagination or from the records themselves—which can be found in many places—in medieval records of Satanists gatherings and ceremonies kept by churches from the consumption of time—and by looking for them you can find these details, ever the same, repeated back into history as far as writing was known. Satan was, and is—and will be—a god not dead, but still followed by a legion of creatures with the weapons of the ancient Gods still kept a secret from us of the surface; and from whom we are protected only by those of the depths who have not inherited the strange disease of sunpolared mental mechanism which results in the inverted destructive logic which is the character of the true demon. He is not "just a bad man:" he is a thing whose every mental process results invariably in a demoniac resolve, a completely unobstructed intent, to do some injury to life which is not as he is.

THERE are several of these feasts of the Demons during the year, but only one Sabbath—the greatest of them all. These people gathered here are those who are the modern descendants of the people responsible in the past for all the wool put in surface men's heads. They pranked and played the devil for the surface man, and laughed at us—and then went to their own feast of the Sabbath and laughed not at all before the awful statue of the God of evil himself. They behaved like witches with their solidograph projectors, wafted surface women around on broom sticks with the ancient levitation beams, and tweaked the bottoms of the Christian priests on the surface in much the same way they had deviled the Greek pagans of Athens and toward as foolish and futile ends.

Witches and warlocks of a mighty kind they might seem to surface men when they played their pranks over the tremendous old miracle rays that were almost their only real contact with the surface; but in the caves they were the dupes of rulers who used them solely because they could be used to kill people who got in their way and not demand payment; who could be used to curse a man who was ambitious, for if told to follow and torment any person from a distance with their ray mech they would do so, "not for a day, not for a year, but always" for their stupidity is of a single-mindedness not understandable to any who do not know the nature of the demon.

The dero is peculiar to the caves, and has to be seen and known for a long period, lived with to be understood or believed in. The stupidity of a creature that looks like a man, has many of man's supposedly divine attributes, yet in truth cannot think much better than a chicken, is a thing hard to believe until you see it for yourself. The dero is the slave of evil thought.

In the caverns, the intelligent men know what evil is, for they can see it in the dero, and know that only degenerate men are evil. On the surface the legend of the cunning and wisdom of evil is still believed in too greatly because we are not acquainted first hand with the thing as it is in persons of hereditarily evil families.

Unfortunately these families, well known for their stupidity and evil life, are not so easily disposed of as might be thought, because a ray position built and weaponed by a God of the Elder race can not be taken even though defended by the veriest fool—because ray of a range sufficient to outrange the ray in fixed position just isn't portable.

Thus the stupid evil demon of the caves lives on because of the invulnerability of the ancient ray positions where he lives for centuries, inviolate and completely destructive of all good in the life under the range of the ancient ray he has inherited through no virtue of his own. There he lives as the dupe and unpaid worker of the Ray-master; and his art consists of being unctuously useful to the slightest whim of his master, and as nasty to the rest of the world as possible. The dupe, the evil unpaid staff-servant, is the custom of the caves; and their numbers are replenished from the "banned" (banshee), the poor mad ones who populate thinly the less desirable reaches of the endless caverns. These have been cast out of the settled, city groups, because too mad or too diseased to live with; but they have children and somehow the children sometimes grow up— in unnamable degradation and conditions of such shame as no surface people can understand.

Still these children grow up and are not always evil, but often *are* evil. These mad nomads have their religions, and the greatest of these is the worship of Satan; but they have also the "white" magic, the "helpers", and many of them serve these as I do, as well as we may. Men like Bonur have their uses for these evil savages of the far, unknown caverns reaches, and cultivate them by such atrocities as this Feast of the Sabbath.

THE people of the cities are not like the savage and hereditarily evil dwellers in the less settled portions of the caves, except in some cities where evil rules entire. In the better cities such men as Brack have carried down the art of repairing the ancient mechanisms, kept alive a science of a mighty kind, the study of the ancient mech, for sale to the highest bidder.

If their stock is looted by some avaricious boss like Bonur, they set out into the endless caverns and come back with many truckloads, many rollats, loaded down with the intricate and tremendously valuable ancient mech, and after repairing it and cleansing the surface of its ages of corrosion—which is very little due to the nature of the metals they use, much of the mech being sheathed in gold—are again in business.

Ships sometimes come from space to buy their wares, and the Lords have always a need of these men, to repair and service their own arsenal of antique weapons, and so do support and protect them in their trade to some extent.

In the cities (cities are really very few in population, the life in the caves is not so numerous as our own—nor so fertile of children), too, live the miners of precious stones, the strippers of gold from the sheathings of the ancient mechanisms, and miners of precious ores who work the vast deep borings of the

Elders' mines, many of which are still worked today after all these dark centuries.

Some of this bullion reaches the surface, and some of the smaller gems, too. But the best of their trade is with the occasional ships from space that have come for their gold since early times. They give in return slaves and merchandise, tools and food, and strange machines of their own from some far planet where life is very different. But these, too, must agree to keep the ancient compact not to tell the surface men anything of the caverns, for their riches are wholly for some of the antique families who still hold the ancient entrances against us—their brothers on the surface—just as they did in the time of the Pharaohs, when they feared we would usurp and rob them of their ancient and invaluable prerogatives, their harems and slaves—and then today of course, there is the bugaboo of a surface "income tax collector". No small fear, either. If they were different in their aims and in their accomplishments for us of the surface I would be the last to expose them to such dangers from our own none too wonderful life and customs. But the good ones of the caves need our help, and I for one would like to see them get it; though how this may come about is a question.

THE idea of extreme stupidity coupled with extreme evil in the same man-beast has no surface parallel but the Nazi, and the motives of the German beast have almost been understandable—but the motivations of these…

Picture the motivation of a thing which has no appetite for love, who cannot desire any gentle pleasure, but does desire the opportunity to be cruel, to see blood flow, to eat human flesh, whose whole soul has been replaced, in the whole heritage of blood, by a robot's desire to please the master. This is a thing of a degraded spirit too low for surface man to comprehend except he has experienced them for years. To see a feast prepared especially to gratify all the dark abysmal appetites of this beast of the ever-night of the caves under our feet—this dark abyss of human evil known to us by legend as Hell—to describe it for those who have not seen it is another thing. I will try.

In Pottstown, Pa. one Johnny Bratton dropped dead of heart failure. There had been nothing apparently wrong with Johnny, in fact he had passed a stiff insurance examination just the week before. Everyone was mystified. His young wife was taken with convulsions from grief, lost the child in her womb. His little daughter of seven was inconsolable over Johnny's death, lost weight, nearly died.

Poison was a weapon little used or thought of in the caverns, just as the ray weapons from the caverns are an unused weapon on the surface and an unbelievable idea to most surface people. A murderer on the surface thinks first of a gun, then of poison. A murderer in the caverns thinks first of a ray bolt, then of some other little known and unsuspected use of the ancient rays for the purpose. Usually this murder takes the form of simulating some disease with the facile ancient rays. Often this is a ray upon the lungs which rots away the lung tissue, makes it appear as a lung disease—or a burn in the heart which doctors call heart failure for want of a way to say the truth. Slow poison was not thought of because they are an ignorant people in the ways of medicine and chemistry; a good clerk from a dispensary of sodas could have disposed of the lot of them.

In the caves under Pottstown, a brainless young ghoul laughed and laughed. He had raised hob with Johnny Bratton, hadn't he? He bragged to his companions, crouched like himself about the great old machine they had used to kill Johnny Bratton.

Over three states the influenza raged. It had assumed the proportions of a plague. Over half the United States the flu spread, area by area. The population was reduced a million or so in a couple of years.

Down in the caves a group of nomad ray people was enjoying their new-old game of imitating influenza with the detrimental ray beams. They laughed as the surface people noted that the flu took only the best and strongest, the most loved people. Others had a mild, non-fatal attack. How could they be so stupid as not to know what the disease really was?

It was particularly funny when the death pained a great many—when the person was well beloved. The old devil tradition was blazing strongly in them as the plague moved slowly across the States, and under the plague rolled their caravan of ancient rollats, bearing their gypsy-like living equipment. It was so easy to put a detrimental ray on a person suffering a mild attack of genuine flu, and watch the disease mount thru his weakened body. It took but a few shots of detrimental ray to make a man so weak he died of the disease.

When one city was finished and most of the love and beauty, the human ties of the city, had been obliterated, the band moved on to decimate another city.

THEIR motivation? It is an old idea they have, they are weakening the people of the surface because they are going to come up to the surface and rule them when they are too weak to fear. But the mad ones of the caves never do come up. The obstacles of moving all their machinery to the surface are too great for their un-technical minds; and they plan it, only to drop the plan after some such orgy of killing the surface men.

In a little town called Stowe, the ex-priest Cachon, a Basque who knew a great deal about devils, came out of a wood where he had been hiding near his home. He had been hiding from the devils, something unseen that tormented him, plucking at his mind with evil thoughts, and at his flesh with evil fingers of pain.

Now the devils finally possessed him and he killed a little girl. The priest was sure the little girl was a "devil".

The priest was confined to the asylum for life. Down below Stowe, the devil ray laughed to "fix" a Christian priest so neatly. Many things happen to priests, very strange things, for the devil ray has an ancient and ingrained antipathy for all Christianity.

But for real fun they prefer to drive a college professor out of his wits with fantastic projections he cannot explain or dare to mention to others, for fear of the madhouse or at least the loss of his job. "Is that *fun!*"

Another trick they delight in is getting a priest on the operating table and then take control of the operating surgeon; "ah, how the 'cloth' slaps the hospital table!" It does not matter that the surgeon goes mad, and the priest dies of his mutilations. It is such fun!

During the period of time the preparation of the feast in the Stem went on—the census takers passed through Ontal, beginning the twice yearly census. The census consisted of taking stock of a man's value for some months to come. If he wasn't valuable in a taxable way, he went to the slave block, or if he wasn't healthy enough for that, he went to a little spoken of but much feared place from which no one ever returned. It was odd that next door to this place of death was a canned meat factory, for there is little meat in the underworld to can.

It was pitiful to hear the mothers list their young daughters as a valuable commodity, to keep from losing them entirely. It was pitiful to hear the destitute promise to find treasure soon, note the hope of finding something of value, some hidden store of the valuable old mech for the masters, something overlooked by the centuries of searchers—for with it they could buy freedom.

THE cult is not a "revival" of the centuries-old worship of Satan, but a continuation of the oldest still-operative religion of earth—the worship of the Spirit of Evil—a church which has functioned in the underworld since before Egypt, so near as I can learn.

The figure of Satan was a great robot, which was activated occasionally by the leaders of the cult—those who traditionally wore the devil masks at the feast—mad sadists in the worst way. For Satanists are hereditary sadists. Once, perhaps, their natural characters were altered into evil by some perverted use of the powerful mind-current rays, but so long had such work gone on that the demon character became an hereditary one. Their ancestors might have been coerced and reconstructed mentally by the ancient Demonists of the centuries of the dark ages, but that darkness still survives in such organizations in the Masked World, and the character of the demon is now an hereditary and unchanged curse of earth. These demonists must have their torment to watch or be most unhappy and ill-adjusted mentally as any good psychologist would know.

The custom of eating human flesh was an ancient one in the underworld. It was revived occasionally. Sometimes by necessity, but oftener in such ceremonies as these bloody ones of this particular survival of the ancient and evil worship of Satan. The Satanist religion, the same that in Medieval times threatened to eclipse the church (though Christian records never admit it). That Satan did not win over our Christian church proves nothing except that the Satanists failed to offer more, failed to protect and value their followers as highly as the Christians, though neither of them were particularly noted for rich rewards for services rendered.

And there you have the TRUTH about the caves, and about my stories. What are you going to DO about it?

Richard S. Shaver

If you've enjoyed this book, you will not want to miss these terrific titles...

ARMCHAIR SCI-FI & HORROR DOUBLE NOVELS, $12.95 each

D-51 **A GOD NAMED SMITH** by Henry Slesar
WORLDS OF THE IMPERIUM by Keith Laumer

D-52 **CRAIG'S BOOK** by Don Wilcox
EDGE OF THE KNIFE by H. Beam Piper

D-53 **THE SHINING CITY** by Rena M. Vale
THE RED PLANET by Russ Winterbotham

D-54 **THE MAN WHO LIVED TWICE** by Rog Phillips
VALLEY OF THE CROEN by Lee Tarbell

D-55 **OPERATION DISASTER** by Milton Lesser
LAND OF THE DAMNED by Berkeley Livingston

D-56 **CAPTIVE OF THE CENTAURIANESS** by Poul Anderson
A PRINCESS OF MARS by Edgar Rice Burroughs

D-57 **THE NON-STATISTICAL MAN** by Raymond F. Jones
MISSION FROM MARS by Rick Conroy

D-58 **INTRUDERS FROM THE STARS** by Ross Rocklynne
FLIGHT OF THE STARLING by Chester S. Geier

D-59 **COSMIC SABOTEUR** by Frank M. Robinson
LOOK TO THE STARS by Willard Hawkins

D-60 **THE MOON IS HELL!** by John W. Campbell, Jr.
THE GREEN WORLD by Hal Clement

ARMCHAIR SCIENCE FICTION CLASSICS, $12.95 each

C-16 **THE SHAVER MYSTERY, Book Three**
by Richard S. Shaver

C-17 **THE GIRLS FROM PLANET 5**
by Richard Wilson

C-18 **THE FOURTH "R"**
by George O. Smith

ARMCHAIR SCIENCE FICTION & HORROR GEMS SERIES, $12.95 each

G-5 **SCIENCE FICTION GEMS, Vol. Three**
C. M. Kornbluth and others

G-6 **HORROR GEMS, Vol. Three**
August Derleth and others

If you've enjoyed this book, you will not want to miss these terrific titles…

ARMCHAIR SCI-FI, FANTASY, & HORROR DOUBLE NOVELS, $12.95 each

D-21 **EMPIRE OF EVIL** by Robert Arnette
THE SIGN OF THE TIGER by Alan E. Nourse & J. A. Meyer

D-22 **OPERATION SQUARE PEG** by Frank Belknap Long
ENCHANTRESS OF VENUS by Leigh Brackett

D-23 **THE LIFE WATCH** by Lester Del Rey
CREATURES OF THE ABYSS by Murray Leinster

D-24 **LEGION OF LAZARUS** by Edmond Hamilton
STAR HUNTER by Andre Norton

D-25 **EMPIRE OF WOMEN** by John Fletcher
ONE OF OUR CITIES IS MISSING by Irving Cox

D-26 **THE WRONG SIDE OF PARADISE** by Raymond F. Jones
THE INVOLUNTARY IMMORTALS by Rog Phillips

D-27 **EARTH QUARTER** by Damon Knight
ENVOY TO NEW WORLDS by Keith Laumer

D-28 **SLAVES TO THE METAL HORDE** by Milton Lesser
HUNTERS OUT OF TIME by Joseph E. Kelleam

D-29 **RX JUPITER SAVE US** by Ward Moore
BEWARE THE USURPERS by Geoff St. Reynard

D-30 **SECRET OF THE SERPENT** by Don Wilcox
CRUSADE ACROSS THE VOID by Dwight V. Swain

ARMCHAIR SCIENCE FICTION CLASSICS, $12.95 each

C-7 **THE SHAVER MYSTERY, Book One**
by Richard S. Shaver

C-8 **THE SHAVER MYSTERY, Book Two**
by Richard S. Shaver

C-9 **MURDER IN SPACE** by David V. Reed
by David V. Reed

ARMCHAIR MASTERS OF SCIENCE FICTION SERIES, $16.95 each

M-3 **MASTERS OF SCIENCE FICTION, Vol. Three**
Robert Sheckley, "The Perfect Woman" and other tales

M-4 **MASTERS OF SCIENCE FICTION, Vol. Four**
Mack Reynolds, "Stowaway" and other tales

If you've enjoyed this book, you will not want to miss these terrific titles…

ARMCHAIR SCI-FI, FANTASY, & HORROR DOUBLE NOVELS, $12.95 each

D-41   **FULL CYCLE** by Clifford D. Simak
            IT WAS THE DAY OF THE ROBOT by Frank Belknap Long

D-42   **THIS CROWDED EARTH** by Robert Bloch
            REIGN OF THE TELEPUPPETS by Daniel Galouye

D-43   **THE CRISPIN AFFAIR** by Jack Sharkey
            THE RED HELL OF JUPITER by Paul Ernst

D-44   **PLANET OF DREAD** by Dwight V. Swain
            WE THE MACHINE by Gerald Vance

D-45   **THE STAR HUNTER** by Edmond Hamilton
            THE ALIEN by Raymond F. Jones

D-46   **WORLD OF IF** by Rog Phillips
            SLAVE RAIDERS FROM MERCURY by Don Wilcox

D-47   **THE ULTIMATE PERIL** by Robert Abernathy
            PLANET OF SHAME by Bruce Elliot

D-48   **THE FLYING EYES** by J. Hunter Holly
            SOME FABULOUS YONDER by Phillip Jose Farmer

D-49   **THE COSMIC BUNGLARS** by Geoff St. Reynard
            THE BUTTONED SKY by Geoff St. Reynard

D-50   **TYRANTS OF TIME** by Milton Lesser
            PARIAH PLANET by Murray Leinster

ARMCHAIR SCIENCE FICTION CLASSICS, $12.95 each

C-13   **SUNKEN WORLD**
            by Stanton A. Coblentz

C-14   **THE LAST VIAL**
            by Sam McClatchie, M. D.

C-15   **WE WHO SURVIVED (THE FIFTH ICE AGE)**
            by Sterling Noel

ARMCHAIR MASTERS OF SCIENCE FICTION SERIES, $16.95 each

MS-5   **MASTERS OF SCIENCE FICTION, Vol. Five**
            Winston K. Marks—Test Colony and other tales

MS-6   **MASTERS OF SCIENCE FICTION, Vol. Six**
            Fritz Leiber—Deadly Moon and other tales

CPSIA information can be obtained
at www.ICGtesting.com
Printed in the USA
FFHW021254260419
52071846-57450FF